IF I HAD

A

HAMMER

IF I HAD A HAMMER

A
HAMMER

A
Swinging
Sixties
Mystery

Teresa Trent

This is book is dedicated to all who lost their Camelot on November 22, 1963.

Praise for If I Had a Hammer

"In Teresa Trent's second book for the Swinging Singles Series, she once again offers a unique story with an engaging cast of characters. Dot Morgan, devasted after witnessing a presidential assassination, steps into a new job, and loses a trusted ally while remaining innocent and flexing to understand the opportunities 1963 offers women. A must-read for any reader who enjoys stepping back into the 'swinging sixties.'"—Terry Korth Fischer, author of the Rory Naysmith Mystery Series

"In author Teresa Trent's If I Had a Hammer, President John F. Kennedy's shocking 1963 assassination triggers a sea change in a young eye-witness. Returning to a small-town secretarial job, the heroine becomes entangled in local murder investigations. While trying to solve the crimes, she realizes new possibilities and potential. This mystery's a nostalgic treat for babyboomers."—Linda Lovely, author of the HOA Mysteries

"Mix great music, bellbottoms, and counterculture in with one of the most turbulent times in American history for a groovy setting full of peace, love, and of course, a murder that turns secretary, Dot Morgan's life upside down. She has to solve the mystery before someone else ends up dead. Trent's latest, If I Had a Hammer, the second in her Swinging Sixties Mysteries, is a twisty mystery and a fun trip back to a generation that changed everything."—Heather Weidner, author of the Jules Keene Glamping Mysteries and the Mermaid Bay Christmas Shoppe Mysteries

Characters

- Dot Morgan, secretary at Gibson Construction
- Ellie Monroe, owner of Bluebonnet Fashions/Dot's cousin
- Jimmy Gibson, part owner of Gibson Construction
- Milton Gibson, part owner of Gibson Construction
- Harry Gibson, father of Jimmy, stepfather of Milton, part owner of Gibson Construction
- Elwood Kirk, Gibson Construction Foreman
- Isabella Gibson, nurse, wife of Milton, mother of Freddie
- Arturo Galvez, owns a company that provides services like plumbing and electric
- Arlene Clark, retired
- Officer Sprague, policeman
- Opal Morgan, Dot's mother/librarian
- Officer Jerry. policeman
- Mary Oliva, policewoman/records clerk
- Ben Dalton, reporter for the Camden Courier
- Charlie Columbo, owner/operator of Columbo's Diner
- Al Maxwell . Ellie's longtime boyfriend and an electrician
- Agnes Gibson, wife of Harry, mother of Milton
- Freddie Gibson, son of Milton and Isabella Gibson

Chapter One

"Turn right here." Ellie held up the Dallas Times-Herald and pointed to a map printed on the front page and directed our taxi driver to Elm Street. Traffic in Dallas was heavy, and all Ellie and I could see in front of us were the taillights of Chevy and Ford sedans. There was a carnival atmosphere about the town. From toddlers to old men, everyone was smiling as they waited for the popular president and his glamorous wife.

"Coming in to see the president? It should be quite a show. I heard it was going to be on the east side of town at the Women's Building. "Good setup over there. Not sure why they moved it over here. Maybe after cancelling Chicago a few weeks ago, they're trying to get it perfect in Dallas." I looked at the rearview mirror and saw the driver's bushy eyebrows go up. "I hear Jackie is with him."

"Yes," I answered, excitement trembling in my voice. Because the temperature outside was in the low sixties, I brought a white sweater to wear over my light pink sleeveless shift. The hemline was shorter than I was used to, hitting just above the knee, and I felt worldly in it. I may have been from a small town in Texas, but today I was rubbing elbows with governors and presidents. I gazed out the open window as couples, families, and reporters found their places along the street, all there for the same reason. We would get to see the president of the United States. After seeing him on TV and hearing him on the radio all this time, it was hard to believe he

1

was an actual person. He was the first president I'd ever voted for. John Fitzgerald Kennedy had been a breath of fresh air in government and put forward programs for civil rights, space exploration, and so many things I believed in.

"Ooh, Dot," Ellie squealed as she bent her bony frame to put her head out the window. The gathers in her wide skirt, an effort to hide her thin frame, bounced up behind her. "I can't believe we're doing this. Start looking for a good spot to stand."

My friend, Mary Oliva, had wanted to come along but couldn't get away from the police station back in Camden. But last night, we talked about what a great day this would be for Dallas, and our optimism for the country. After a long line of presidents who just played politics, we saw Kennedy as the first one in a long time to bring hope for the future. Mary was particularly grateful for his willingness to take on civil rights, something desperately needed for all races. For once, things were going right.

Ellie screamed, making the driver jump. "Right here! Stop here," Ellie said as she passed bills from the back seat to the front.

I looked up over a light brown building with straight white letters reading Texas School Book Depository. Above it was an ad for Hertz Rent-a-Car with a clock attached to it. It was straight up noon. The crowd was thickening as people found places to stand in a grassy area next to the street. It was almost as if the original landscaper had known this historic day would take place and designed the gradual slope along the road. According to the newspaper, Kennedy's motorcade would arrive soon, and I felt the excitement building as we prepared to join the crowd. I pulled my arms through my sweater.

Ellie extended a hand to help me out of the yellow Checker cab. "Are you ready?"

"Oh yes. Let's go over there." I pointed to one of the few open spots next to the curb. "Hurry before someone else gets it. I just hope we can hold the spot. There are some pretty big guys who might want to stand in front of us."

Ellie smirked. "You know what I always say. 'Knee them in the crotch, and they sing a new song.'"

2

"Seriously, Ellie. I'm not attacking some poor man just so I can stand in front."

"You're right. I was trying to sound sophisticated. Maybe not here, but remember that. It may come in handy someday."

I had decided to wear a new pair of black heels and felt them wobbling. We crossed the street and grabbed our spot just in time, causing another viewer to crowd in next to us. The smell of cigarette smoke circled us as people fiddled with cameras and readjusted black-rimmed glasses.

"Jack Kennedy is so handsome." Ellie placed her hand over her heart, popping it on her chest like a heartbeat. "Too bad he's already taken."

"Stop." I laughed. "I believe you're already taken as well. Didn't I hear something about you and Al getting married next June?"

Ellie gave a sweet smile as her eyes drifted upward. "I can't believe that either. June. That's just a little more than six months away."

"Well, you deserve the happiness coming your way." I patted my cousin's shoulder. Ellie was in her thirties, practically spinsterhood in 1963. Finding Al, the electrician, had been the best thing for her. Love and marriage. It filled me with warmth. We were all living the American dream, just like the characters in our favorite movies at the Rialto theater. The lyrics of "Young at Heart" drifted through my mind.

I sang a few lines from the song.

Ellie linked her arm with mine as she watched the street. A few cars drove by, but none that looked like a presidential motorcade. The breeze drifted across my exposed knees. A longer skirt would have shielded my knees, but I would endure the shivers for the sake of fashion.

"Ellie, did you see that picture of Jackie in the paper? She's gorgeous. I saw her tour of the White House on TV. She's so classy and looks beautiful in everything she wears."

"Except she talks funny," Ellie said, her Texas drawl turning "talks" into "tawks."

"That's because she's from the East. She can't help it. I'll bet she thinks Texans talk funny. I'm sure they hear a lot of Texas twang coming from LBJ and Ladybird."

"But that's just music to anyone's ears," Ellie said. "Be serious."

I glanced up and down the parade route. "Ben said he was going to be here. Maybe he's farther down the street." I pulled out my new Kodak Instamatic and hooked the leather strap around my neck. I raised the camera up to my eyes. "I hope I can get a clear picture of Jackie and John."

"Listen to you. You talk like you know them," Ellie laughed. "Jackie and John."

"Well, in a way, I feel like I do. They're America's perfect family. I love them all. Jackie, John, Caroline, John-John."

Ellie sighed and then drew in an excited breath with her hands clenched in front of her. "This is so exciting." People continued to crowd up to the curb. A tall man in a brown plaid sport coat, holding binoculars up to his boxy black glasses, elbowed me to move over. I could feel tension in the air that comes when people anticipate witnessing something spectacular.

Just then, a line of shiny black cars came into view, ambling down the street in our direction. The breeze turned into a slight wind. I leaned forward and squinted, trying to identify who was in each vehicle. I felt my heart race as I recognized John and Jackie Kennedy sitting in the back seat as the car was surrounded by men on motorcycles. She was stunning in a pink wool suit and matching hat. I felt special knowing Jackie and I had worn the same color on this memorable day. She, of course, looked so much better. John had a healthy tan and a wide smile on his face.

I raised my camera and willed the man in the brown plaid coat not to step in front of me. This was a moment I was sure we would always remember. I hoped I could wind the film cartridge fast enough to take several pictures. Maybe they would want to use them in the *Camden Courier*? I wanted a good one of John, and another of Jackie. Just like real people, I thought, but really, they looked like royalty, sitting in the open top limousine with policemen on motorcycles riding silently alongside—sort of a mobile palace guard. When the hood of the limousine was directly in front of me, I brought the Instamatic up and clicked to take a picture. I rolled the film to the next frame, took another, and repeated the process. Suddenly, I heard a popping sound somewhere behind me. I rolled the film lever with my thumb, now an automatic action, then turned toward the sound, only to see people scrambling and running to higher ground. The sound I heard wasn't a pop. It was a gunshot. I looked back toward the motorcade and stood in horror as a man crawled over the back of the open convertible, and the thing that caught my attention was the splotches of red invading Jackie's beautiful pink suit. John Kennedy no longer sat smiling in front of me but was down in the seat on Jackie's lap.

The car sped up and out of view. Somewhere in the moment Ellie had pulled me down, and my knees dug in where the ground was cold and wet. We heard screams all around us. Ellie yelled, "We have to get away from the street. Come on." She yanked my arm, nearly tearing the white sweater off me. The whole scene had turned to chaos, but one thing I knew for sure—the president had been hit.

Chapter Two

One Week Later

As I sat behind my desk on Friday morning, I caught a tear on my cheek, the tears still coming days later.

Milton Gibson, my boss's brother, stood next to my desk and set down a new thermos. He was especially proud of it because it was a gift from his wife to congratulate him on a new demolition project his family's business, Gibson Construction, was in the process of completing. He gazed at me and my tears. "You should take a sick day, Dot. Believe me, I know. Seeing something like that is no different than being in a war. It's hard to work when you've been through something that traumatic."

Milton, a thinly built man in his thirties, still wore the military crew cut even though he was no longer in the service. He had served as a military advisor in Vietnam for three years with his best friend, John Oliva. Milton was also married to John's sister, Isabella, a beautiful woman with jet-black hair that flowed past her shoulders. The two were mismatched. He had a kind face, but would never be a Paul Newman, while she was a statuesque beauty. I had often wondered where the attraction was between the two, but it was clearly there because they were happily married and had a seven-year-old little boy named Freddie.

My first job had come through this union. I met Milton at a barbecue John and Mary hosted, and he offered me the position. I was over the moon to be working in my first job out of secretarial school, until I discovered Gibson

Construction was run by *two* brothers. One was nice, and one was trouble.

"I'm okay. It's just we were so close to it all. Seeing a news story is one thing, but being in the middle of one is horrible. All I could think about was getting to see John Kennedy. He was so handsome, and seeing Jackie was like seeing a movie star." A tear formed, and I blew into my tissue. "Now I wish we'd never gone."

Milton spoke softly. "It takes time to get over something like this. Try to focus on just getting through today."

"Ellie closed the dress shop for the whole week. She was really shaken up. If it hadn't been for her pulling me up the hill, I might have been shot." Closing Blue Bonnets for the entire week prior to Thanksgiving with so many Christmas orders that needed sewing was quite a sacrifice for Ellie. While I had been looking through the lens of my Instamatic, Ellie had been looking directly at President Kennedy. She saw him get shot. Now Ellie kept to herself, not talking, not sewing, not anything. "I can't believe Mr. Gibson decided to open today," I said. "Half of the businesses in town shut their doors until next week in observance of the president's death."

Milton raised an eyebrow as he poured coffee from his new thermos. "You know he's been waiting for this day for months. Nothing is going to slow down the first day of demolition. That's just the way he is, but don't worry. I think I have some news that'll put him in a good mood today."

"Good." I wiped at my eyes.

"What's good?" Jimmy Gibson bustled through the door and removed his red and brown plaid jacket, and hung it up on pegs by the door. He looked nothing like his brother. He was shorter than Milton, and stocky. His full cheeks were ruddy from hours spent working outside. But Jimmy and Milton were related by marriage only. Milton's mother married Jimmy's father who then adopted Milton to give both boys the same name.

"Good morning, Mr. Gibson," I said.

He hustled to his desk, absorbed in his morning routine, my tears unseen. "I was at the bank finishing up the paperwork for the new strip mall. We're ready to start. Strip malls are where it's at. There'll come a time when shopping downtown will be a thing of the past."

Gibson Construction had been acquiring empty lots and homes to make room for stores and a large parking area. Jimmy himself owned one of the homes which he kept as a rental property, and his father owned the others. Almost all the homeowners received fat checks to vacate in a hurry. It had taken him over a year to acquire the property, but now it was ready.

"So, what's the good news?" Jimmy asked.

"I've been a busy little bee during our time off after the assassination." Milton approached Jimmy's desk and pulled up a chair.

"I'm listening, but don't have much time, so get to it." One thing I quickly learned after starting this job was that Jimmy considered time to be money. He rushed everywhere and had no patience with anything his brother Milton did or said.

"I did some of the erstwhile demolition on the project." Jimmy began to protest, but Milton held up a hand. "On my own time, so don't worry about that."

"That wasn't necessary."

"Well, I did. I worked on the lot of your old rental house. I'm surprised you didn't see it on your way in this morning."

Jimmy gave a quick eyebrow raise and then scowled. "Like I said, that wasn't necessary."

"I'm trying to carry my weight around here. If the Army taught me nothing else, it taught me the importance of hard work and a job well done. Besides, we can't let Sawyer take the Golden Hammer."

Each year the city of Camden awarded one construction company the Golden Hammer in recognition of projects that improved the look and economy of our town. Gibson Construction had won the award two years in a row but was getting some stiff competition this year from Sawyer Home Builders.

"Well, okay." Jimmy gave a slow nod. "How, uh, far did you get?"

"Pretty far on one side. Oh, and before I forget, I found this." Milton squirmed a little to pull a tiny gold chain with a heart on it out of his pocket. The necklace was tarnished and dirty, but with a little cleaning would be wearable.

Jimmy took the necklace from Milton. "Why would you give this to me? You could have just thrown it in a trash can for all I care."

"I know, but there was just something about it that made it look valuable. I'll bet that's real gold. I thought you might like to have it. It was on your property."

Jimmy reached over and dropped the dingy necklace in the trash. "Well, that's where you're wrong. It's trash."

Milton looked down at his fingernails, appearing disappointed his big surprise was not well received.

"I know you thought it was a good idea to get a jump on the job, but I'd prefer you worked under my time and supervision."

Milton had wanted to surprise his brother with his dedication to the job and the found treasure, but Jimmy didn't seem to care. Milton's shoulders slumped. I looked at the clock. It was 8:45. Only seven hours and fifteen minutes to go.

Jimmy had scheduled a staff photo at the demolition site, so at least that would be fun. I grabbed my purse out of the bottom drawer of my desk.

Milton came over, holding his thermos under one arm and a spare hard hat in the other hand. "Here, Dot. My wife wouldn't speak to me if I didn't make sure you were safe."

"Thanks," I said, hoping it wouldn't crush my hairdo.

When we got to the site, things were buzzing, and even better, Ben Dalton, a reporter from the *Camden Courier*, lumbered over. He was a tall, lanky man who was almost always seen in a trench coat and fedora. He looked more like a G-man than a reporter. Gibson Construction's demolition project wasn't breaking news, but people love to watch buildings come down, and Jimmy believed any publicity was good publicity.

Ben smiled at me. "How are you doing?"

"Fine, I guess. I'm glad you didn't make it to Dallas on Friday."

"Me, too. Even though I'll probably regret missing that story for the rest of my life."

Milton nodded. "We'll never be the same, but today we turn a block into a field, and I guess life goes on."

"I guess so." I felt a chill run through me.

Based on the crowd gathering across the street, this demolition apparently qualified as a major event in Camden. Arlene Clark, my landlady, waved her white gloves when we looked her direction. This demolition was a big deal for the town. It signaled progress, and rumor was that Sears and Roebuck was coming in. We were in the nineteen sixties now, and according to Jimmy that meant a future filled with retail shopping and more choices currently only found in Dallas. Now Camden would be on the edge of fashion and retail.

In the interest of progress, a row of four houses would be demolished, starting with Jimmy's tiny one-bedroom rental property that he'd owned for years. The rest of the homes were a little bigger, but also rental properties. The tenants of these houses were mostly the families of roughnecks who worked in the oil fields. I had memories of seeing children playing in these yards where grass had forgotten to grow, and washing machines stood proudly on the front porches. Now, most of the sidewalks had been broken up with a jackhammer. The clotheslines had disappeared, and the demolition crew was circling around like a flock of buzzards. Elwood Kirk, the foreman, towered over his men as he directed them to various tasks.

"I'll bet this is much more exciting than typing and filing," Ben said in a low voice. He snapped a picture of the machines ready for work.

"It sure is." I felt for the tiny gold heart necklace in my pocket. As soon as Jimmy had left the office, I'd fished the necklace out of the trash can. It looked like such a pretty piece, I was curious if it could be cleaned up. I only had time to brush the dirt off, but once we were done with this PR event, I'd go back and polish it up. It was well made and not something you would expect a person of little means to have. It must have been a cherished keepsake of one renter.

"All right, everybody," Jimmy blared through a bullhorn, "you'll need to step back a bit. You don't want to get hit by flying debris." He motioned for us to stand across the street with the rest of the onlookers.

Before I could cross, Jimmy placed a hand on my arm. "Have you seen Milton? He's supposed to be doing this."

I glanced around, but no longer saw Milton among the hard hats. "He was here a minute ago."

"Great. When we need him to do his job, he disappears," Jimmy muttered. "I'll have to clear the site myself." He raised a hand, signaling Elwood, the crew foreman, who had climbed into the shiny excavator.

"Your boss wasn't too happy," Ben said, snapping another picture that would undoubtedly be labeled "Before" in the paper.

"He seldom is," I admitted.

"Fun job."

As we found our place in the crowd across the street, Jimmy gave a swirling motion with his hand to signal Elwood to begin the demolition. The bucket of the golden JCB 100 excavator jutted over to the roof of Jimmy's rent house and pounded into the roof. It took out shingles that had kept out the rain, cracked glass, and tore through siding. The little house began to come down. Windows that used to hold curtains, doors painted red, and an upstairs bedroom typical for a couple just starting out. It all came down like memories blowing away in the wind. As the wood and metal turned into piles of rubble, I realized how pretty the trees were behind the houses. Funny how a house makes you forget to look at nature. Working from the center of the house, the bucket was about to take down a first-story overhang when Milton came wandering out, stumbling over pieces of wood dumped by the giant machine.

"Milton? What's wrong with him?" I asked.

Ben picked up his camera and clicked off a shot. "I don't know."

"Milton!" I yelled. "What are you doing?" I ran toward the demolition, waving my hands back and forth toward Elwood on the excavator. He pulled the bucket up and away from Milton, but a large chunk of wood, already loosened by the force of the battering, knocked Milton to the ground. I ran to him and tried to pull the beam off, and was quickly joined by Jimmy, Ben, and some of the crew members.

"What the hell was he doing here?" Jimmy shouted as they heaved the wood off his brother's still body.

Milton didn't move. Jimmy pointed at Elwood, who had come down off the excavator seat. "Get to a phone and call an ambulance," he yelled.

Milton stirred and looked up into my eyes.

"You came! I love you so much, Isabella. I'm the luckiest man—"

"He's out of his head," I said as Milton raised a hand to cup my cheek. I put my hand on his.

"It's me, Dot. Dot Morgan. You're hurt."

"I love you, darling," Milton went on, oblivious to the fact he was talking to the wrong woman. "So beautiful," he slurred.

"Maybe he has a concussion," I said.

Jimmy Gibson smirked. "And maybe he's a damn idiot walking into a demolition in progress like that. Ever since he got married, he's been an idiot, and now he's halted a million-dollar project."

I couldn't believe Jimmy was more worried about the project than his own brother. I wondered how bad it would look on my resume to be at my first job for only one month. This man was heartless.

I glanced over and saw Milton's prized thermos among the rubble, now with a noticeable dent in the side. The gift from his wife—the woman it seems he wanted to have present but who hadn't shown up. When the ambulance drivers arrived, I stepped over and picked up the thermos. I'd return it to Isabella. Milton would want it, he cherished it so. It was a simple gift, but to him, it was important.

Chapter Three

Never one to get off schedule, Jimmy resumed the demolition, even though Milton was on his way to the hospital. His brother's injury didn't seem to be of concern to Jimmy. The crowd dispersed. Ben rushed off to get his pictures developed, leaving me alone on the curb. Jimmy walked over, his face a deep red.

"Go on back to the office to collect any messages from the answering service. I also left you a couple of letters on the Dictaphone. Once you get caught up on that, head on over to the hospital to check on Milton. I can't believe that idiot walked into a demo. Find out how bad he's hurt and when he'll be getting back to work. I need to see if I should hire somebody to replace him."

Jimmy's reaction to Milton's accident caught me off guard. It was bad enough the man wouldn't even go to the hospital to check on his own brother but sent the secretary instead. Even then, I thought he'd want me to pick up flowers or check to see if Milton's wife needed anything, not help Jimmy determine whether he had enough manpower. Of course, some families were different, and Jimmy and Milton were as opposite as day and night. Men fascinated me in the way they reacted to things. I had never seen John Wayne cry in a movie, so maybe Jimmy was trying to be like the matinee cowboy star. I saw nothing wrong with men crying. I'd seen my father cry at the death of his mother and never thought less of him for it, only loved him more.

In the beginning, I thought Jimmy's dedication and ambition were admirable, but now he just struck me as callous. Were all bosses like this?

Why didn't they have a course on bosses in secretarial school?

When I arrived at the hospital, I found Isabella Gibson sitting by Milton's bedside with their son Freddie in her lap. John Oliva, Isabella's brother, sat on the other side of the bed.

Isabella held Milton's hand as he slept. He looked frightening with his bandaged head and off-white skin. He had given me a hard hat for protection, but from the looks of him, they weren't all that effective.

I placed a bouquet on a counter next to the window. "These are from Jimmy. Sorry he couldn't be here, but he didn't want to get the job off schedule. How is Milton doing?"

"The doctor says it's okay for him to sleep. It will rest his brain from the injury. The painkillers have had him sleeping on and off most of the day," Isabella answered in a soft voice. Milton had a wife whose looks could stop traffic with her coal black hair in a braid and her warm brown skin. Freddie had her hair color, but Milton's nose and ready smile.

With all the chairs taken, I stood at the end of the bed. "How bad is it?"

John sat with shoulders slumped as he looked at his best friend. "Not that bad, but they want to observe him for a couple of days. We still don't understand why he was inside that house while the excavator was knocking down the wall. Do you know why?"

My mind flashed back to Milton, stepping out, his eyes unfocused. "I wish I did. I saw him a few minutes before the demolition started but after that, I have no idea where he went."

Isabella reached out and touched Milton's cheek. "I keep thinking he was checking for someone inside the house. That's the only reason I can think of that he would something so unsafe."

Freddie looked up at his mother, fear in his eyes. "Is Daddy going to be all right?"

"Sure he is, baby," Isabella answered, hugging him, and then placing a kiss on his cheek. He hugged her even tighter, and she began to rock him.

John leaned over and spoke in a quiet voice. "Milton and I were in some pretty scary situations in Vietnam, even if we were only military advisors. He was always a careful guy back then. I can't imagine why he would walk around a house that was being torn down. It doesn't make any sense."

Isabella nodded toward the flowers. "That was nice of Jimmy to send flowers, even if he didn't bother to come to the hospital. I guess when he's not your blood brother, the job comes first."

Jimmy sure didn't fool Isabella. She knew I was sent to do his brotherly errand. I gave a weak smile, deciding not to tell Isabella that Jimmy Gibson knew nothing about the flowers. Isabella had enough to deal with right now.

"Jimmy sent me flowers?" Milton muttered from the bed.

Isabella jumped at Milton's words, and Freddie stood. "Thank God. You're awake finally."

Milton turned to her, confusion in his eyes.

"Daddy!" Freddie took his father's hand.

Milton gave Freddie a gentle smile. "Hey, Champ." He looked to Isabella. "How did I get here?"

"You were in an accident at work, remember?" Isabella said. "How does your head feel?"

Milton reached up and touched the bandages wrapped around his head. "That would explain this headache. It feels like somebody hit me with a brick."

"Not quite. It was a wood beam," John corrected.

"I don't understand. I don't remember anything."

I walked closer, hugging my arms to ward off the chill of the hospital. "You were inside the house Elwood was taking down. We can't figure out why you would have been in there."

Milton's eyes searched and found me. "Hi, Dot. How's the demolition going?"

Isabella scowled. "All you can talk about is that job? How about, 'Sorry, Isabella, for almost getting myself killed?'"

His gaze returned to his wife. "Sorry, dear."

"The demolition is going fine, so don't worry about that," I reassured him. "We are all as confused as you are and how you ended up in the middle of that house going down."

Milton gave a blank stare and then took in a breath. "It was a mistake. I don't know. I thought I was at…I don't know."

"Think about it, Milton," John urged. "Were you trying to make sure the house was clear? Were you worried there was somebody in there?"

Milton still looked confused, his eyes downcast, then he looked forward and took a little gasp.

"You remember something?" Isabella asked.

He looked at Isabella, and his neck stiffened. Then he gave a tremulous smile.

"No. Um, I have a splitting headache. Do you think I could get some aspirin?"

John stood. "Sure. I'll go get the nurse." The two men shared a look, and then John strode to the hallway.

Isabella leaned over and kissed Milton's forehead. "I'm only glad you're okay. I was so worried about you."

"I'm sorry. I—" He stopped midsentence. "I'm sorry."

I was happy to see Milton awake but felt like it was time for me to leave. "I'd better get back to work. I'll tell Jimmy you're awake. You might want to give him a call to let him know you're okay." I tried to leave that as a subtle warning. Jimmy's last words about replacing Milton echoed in my mind, but I didn't want to give Milton something else to worry about.

"Thanks, Dot."

"No problem. Get better." With a little wave, I was out the door, my heels clicking down the tiled hallway of the sterile white hospital. As I breathed in the smell of antiseptic, it became achingly clear. Milton was holding something back.

That night, I sat with the two rambunctious Oliva children while Mary and John spent time at the hospital. Mary had left a casserole in the refrigerator which just needed to be reheated in the oven. Before long the smell of peppers and tomato sauce made my stomach growl. I hadn't realized how hungry I was until we settled down in front of the television. Marisol and Joey sat with plates on TV trays, and I turned on *I Love Lucy*. The light fare was better than the many programs and tributes that seemed to be monopolizing TV and radio broadcasts. The speeches, songs, and poems dedicated to JFK were beautiful but made me cry and led to a feeling of hopelessness that kept creeping into my mind.

The antics of Lucy and Ethel did nothing to lighten my spirit. It was as if there wasn't enough air in the room to fill my lungs. For the first time in my life, I felt unhappy, and I wasn't sure why. I was following my dream when I took the job at Gibson Construction. Or was I? I had studied to become a secretary, but why did I feel like it just wasn't enough? I'd had dreams of working in a corporation, being challenged intellectually, and getting the chance to work my way up the corporate ladder. But my dream job came with an explosive boss and long days of tedium.

True to their word, Mary and John came through the door after visiting hours at the hospital ended at eight o'clock.

"Thank you so much for doing this for us. The whole family was there. Well, at least on our side. I'm not sure why his parents weren't there." Mary hung up her coat in the closet off the front hall. "Were the kids okay for you?"

"Yes. No problems."

John's eyes met Mary's, and he grinned. "They must like you."

"You look tired, Dot. I guess you've had a long day, too." Mary missed little. She was a valuable member of the local police department and would be an asset to them if they'd only let her spend more time on criminals and less on filing. Mary had often spoken to me about how being a woman—particularly a woman of Mexican descent—were barriers to her advancement.

"Yes, long day." I let out a sigh as John redirected the kids from the television to their bedtime rituals. I reached for my coat. "Can I ask you something?"

Mary walked over and turned off the TV. "Sure," she said.

"How do you work all day not doing what you hoped to do but being a glorified file clerk?"

"I like to think I'm a little more than that, but I get your point. It's not what I trained for at the academy." She ran her hand through her hair, making shiny black strands fall around her face. "I don't know. I do it. Why do you ask? Are you having second thoughts about your new job?"

I plopped back down on Mary's couch. I could hear a bathtub filling down the hall. "I don't know. I thought I was fine, but ever since the assassination, my life doesn't feel the same."

Mary sat down beside me and took my hand. "I'll bet it doesn't. You were right on top of a horrible, horrible thing. Nobody should see that, especially as close as you were. I'm sure it's something you won't forget for a very long time. If ever."

I drew my lips together and sighed. "But why would that affect how I feel about my job? Before it happened, Jimmy was my boss, end of story. Sure, he was gruff, but that was just Jimmy. But now I see him as pushy and unfeeling. The way he talked about Milton was downright mean."

Mary scowled. "What did he say?"

"He didn't care that Milton got hurt as much as how inconvenient it was that he'd left the construction company a man short."

She scrunched up her nose. "He actually said that?"

"Sort of. I can't believe I'm saying this, but I start my workday and count the hours until I'm finished." I put my head in my hands. "I keep feeling like I made a mistake. I don't want to be a secretary anymore."

"You're tired." Mary rubbed my back, just as I imagine she does for her children when they have a nightmare. "It'll get better."

"You can't promise that."

"I know. But I can hope it for you."

I had to straighten up for Mary. "I'm sorry. You've been worrying about Milton, and here I am talking about my stupid problems."

"You're right. I'm very worried about Milton and how all this will affect Isabella, but there's always time for you, too."

"How was he tonight?"

Mary looked down, and when she raised her eyes, there was wariness in them. "I don't know. He's different, somehow. Isabella said something to him, and he snapped at her. I don't even remember what it was, but it's unusual for Milton to do something like that."

Milton had always been cheerful around me, and to hear he argued with his wife was surprising. "He must be in a lot of pain."

"Sure," Mary agreed.

Chapter Four

After a restful weekend, I typed without thinking on Monday morning. Milton was still in the hospital, and when I visited him, I think he was pretending to be asleep. At least I could listen to the radio while Jimmy was out of the office. I typed along to Peter, Paul, and Mary singing "If I Had a Hammer" and caught myself tapping keys to the beat until I misspelled something. I chuckled at the irony of listening to "If I Had a Hammer" in an office where the Golden Hammer construction award was so coveted. Jimmy and Milton talked about it constantly. As I fumed at the typewriter, tackling the error with my pink eraser wheel, the phone rattled on my desk.

"What are you doing for lunch?" It was Mary.

Eying the folded paper bag on the corner of my desk, I answered. "Eating a peanut butter and jelly sandwich and questioning my career choices."

Mary laughed. "I've been there daily. Isabella sent Arturo Galvez to see Milton this morning." Arturo Galvez owned a service company specializing in plumbing and electric. He had once approached Al, Ellie's boyfriend, to come work for him, but Al liked having his own business and declined the offer.

"Why would she do that? I didn't even know Arturo and Milton were friends."

"He isn't as much Milton's friend as Isabella's. She and Arturo have known each other for years. We always thought he'd be the one she'd marry, not Milton. Then she and Milton had a son, so we knew he was right for her."

"Was Isabella there?"

"No, she had to take John's abuela to the doctor in Dallas and won't be back until later this afternoon. She didn't want Milton left alone all day, so she asked Arturo to go by. She also wanted us to go and check on him."

"Sure. What time?"

"I'll pick you up at noon. Does that work?"

"Yes. Jimmy's out at the demolition all day, so I can take my lunch whenever. I'm typing up invoices and paying bills."

"And now I see why you're examining your career choices."

When I hopped into Mary's car at noon, she smiled. "This was how we met. You shared your lunch with me," I said.

"I had to. I've never seen such a pitiful-looking little Anglo girl. Of course, you surprised me when I found out you were as stubborn as I was."

"As I recall, that was what you liked about me."

"Absolutely."

I ran a finger along the wrinkled brown paper bag that held my lunch. "So, were Arturo and Isabella romantically involved? Why would he be visiting Milton if Isabella weren't there?"

"Who knows? Maybe he's doing it because of his friendship with Isabella."

"I suppose, but when I'm sick, I don't want to talk to people I barely know. Milton seems so off-kilter already."

"I know. And this whole accident makes no sense. He's been around plenty of construction sites, and he's always safety-conscious. What would make him wander under a collapsing structure?"

"Yeah. It's as if he was suffering from temporary insanity."

Mary nodded while keeping her eyes on the road. "I've known Milton for a few years now, and he's a levelheaded guy. He was the best thing that could have ever happened to Isabella. Now I'm wondering if we really know him."

When Mary and I obtained our visitors' passes and stepped into Milton's room, an elderly lady in a pink quilted bed jacket looked up at us. I turned around and checked the room's number—313. The room was right, but the patient was not.

Mary apologized to the startled woman. "We're sorry. The man who was in here must have been moved."

"I've only been here an hour," she said. "Gallbladder."

"Well, then, good luck. I'm sure you'll be fine," I said. I had no idea whether she'd be fine, but it seemed like the thing to say.

Mary and I approached the nurse's station, where two women in crisp white uniforms and bobby-pinned hats sat writing in files.

"Excuse me. Can you tell me where they've moved Milton Gibson?"

One of the freshly starched nurses looked up, raising a long thin nose toward me. "Mr. Gibson," she said, drawing the name out in disgust. "We'd all like to know where he is. He got dressed and walked right out of the hospital about two hours ago." She looked over at her colleague. "Some people will do anything to avoid the bill." She made a clucking sound with her tongue.

"Yep," the other nurse chimed in. "And he seemed like such a nice fella."

"Did he say where he was going?"

"Nope, but something wasn't right. He took off down the hall like he was running from a bill collector."

I looked back at the room. Why had Milton left like that? Who would Milton be running from? His family had money, so I doubted he was running from the bill.

"I'll try to talk to John's dad to see when Isabella is expected back." Mary began buttoning her coat but then stopped. "And then I'd better run into the station to tell them what's going on. If he's out there wandering around with a head injury, they're going to want to know about it."

"Good idea," I agreed. Without a car, he couldn't have gotten far.

"What's a good idea?" Ben appeared from around the corner wearing a rumpled navy suit topped off by his trench coat.

"Milton's gone. Just walked away. We have no idea where he is," I said.

"He left? Without the doctor's permission?" He furrowed his brow. "I came to interview him for a follow-up piece in the paper. Guess I'll have to tell my editor to put that on hold."

"I have to go," Mary said. "Can I drop you back at work?"

Ben raised a finger. "I'd be happy to drive Dot back to work, if you don't mind."

Mary's lips creased into a smile, and she shot me a glance.

"If it isn't too much trouble."

Ben made a bowing motion. "My pleasure."

As Mary's heels clicked down the hall, Ben drew closer. "How much time do you have left for your lunch?"

I checked my Timex. "About forty minutes. Why?"

He looked down at the paper bag I was carrying. "We could look for Milton while you eat your lunch."

"I couldn't ask you to do that. You don't have a lunch."

"I ate before I got here. My mother always said the only thing I show up to on time was meals." He patted his stomach and then continued. "Where do you think he may have gone?"

I rubbed at my eyes with my free hand. "I don't know. He might have gone home. If he did, Mary will find out when she gets there. We could check work."

Ben nodded. "We could, but it's a strange thing to leave the hospital and report for work without telling anybody. What kind of mood has he been in lately?"

I thought back to my last visit with Milton. He seemed very aware, in spite of his injury, but something had been off, and he was anxious about something. The ready smile, the twinkle in his eyes, all gone.

"Milton was acting strangely. He seemed nervous around me."

Ben shrugged. "Well, you are a beautiful woman."

I rolled my eyes and shook my head. "That's nice of you to say, but it wasn't that. He was looking at the door, dropping threads of conversation, and he kept clutching the sheet with his hands. Stuff like that."

"Let's start walking," Ben said, placing a comfortable hand on the small of my back. "Interesting. He wasn't himself and you don't think it was the concussion." He stroked his chin with his other hand. "Did he mention anything?"

"Like what?"

"Like why he was acting that way? Was he afraid his brother was going to find a way to cut him out of the business because of his accident?"

I raised an eyebrow. Ben wasn't off with that one. Jimmy had complained that Milton's carelessness was causing him to miss work and set the project back.

"Jimmy was upset, but you can't fire your own family in a family business."

"Which would make it even more possible that he tried to go back to work. Let's drive by the site." Ben pointed to a beat-up blue Chevy in the parking lot and then opened my door, causing a loud metallic squeak that sent a squirrel running up a tree. When he started the motor, there was a crunching sound that synced in with every gear shift.

When we arrived at the demolition site, there was a noticeable change. The first little house was gone, and most of the debris had been swept up. Jimmy was yelling something to the excavator operator, who had moved on to the second house. Once again, I noticed the towering trees on the property and thought how beautiful they would be with the rich green leaves of summer. Too bad they couldn't leave the lot as it was now. Who needed another shopping mall when the alternative was this? "Do you see him?" Ben asked.

I surveyed the site. "No, I don't see him anywhere, but let's ask Jimmy."

After trudging across the dirt, I waved at Jimmy.

He scowled as I drew nearer. "Is something wrong at the office? You know to use the radio."

"I'm still on lunch break, but we're looking for Milton. He just walked out of the hospital. Have you seen him? Did he come here?"

Jimmy shook his head, gripping his chin in frustration. "My brother is an idiot. No, he's not here. God knows where he is. I don't have time to worry about him right now."

As we made our way back to the car, Ben said, "Okay, let's check your office." We drove the two blocks to the office, and when I unlocked the door, the room was still silent. "Milton?" I called out. No answer. We walked to the back, where the bathroom was, but it was empty.

Ben folded his arms and raised an eyebrow. "Well, that shoots the theory he was anxious to get back to work and save his job."

"Yeah, but now we're back to what he was nervous about."

"I have a crazy hunch. It's what we professional journalists do. Act on hunches." Ben did a U-turn and headed out of the office, his trench coat swishing behind him as he returned to the car.

"Professional journalist, huh? Sounds like you made that up." I followed him and got back in the car.

"No, ma'am. That's what I am, according to Funk and Wagnalls. Look up the word 'reporter,' and you'll see it." He pulled into the parking lot of Camden's bus station. A blue greyhound that lit up at night graced the front of the station as well as the word "Greyhound" in running neon reminded riders as small as we were, we had a bus that could take them to Dallas, or elsewhere.

"You think he got on a bus? Why would he do that?"

"Now, if we knew that, we wouldn't be wandering around wasting your lunch hour. How much time do we have left?"

I checked again. "Ten minutes."

"Great."

We strode into the bus station. The clerk behind the counter was busy reading a tattered copy of the *Police Gazette,* which featured a buxom girl on the cover.

"Excuse me?" Ben asked.

"Where to?" The man set down his magazine and, seeing me, turned the cover to the counter.

"Did you see that guy who walked into a demolition site in the paper?" Ben asked.

"Oh yeah. Not his day, I guess."

This was great. The clerk knew what Milton looked like. I leaned forward on the counter. "Was he here in the last couple of hours?"

The clerk nodded up and down, causing his double chin to triple and then go back to double. "As a matter of fact, he was. He looked like a decent fellow and all, but who goes traipsing around a demolition site? That's about as smart as going down to the beach to watch a tidal wave come in."

Good one. I'd have to remember that. "Did he board a bus?"

"If it was your guy, he was in here a little while ago. Bought a ticket for Denver."

"Colorado?"

"Is there another?" I was sure he'd pegged me as a dumb blonde.

"You have to understand," I said, "he walked out of the hospital with a head injury. We're not sure he knows what he's doing. When does the bus get into Denver?"

The clerk blew out a sigh. "Let me check."

He pulled out a bus chart and ran a finger down a row. "Looks like at four o'clock tomorrow afternoon. Head injury, huh? I could call ahead and make sure they know what's going on. The last thing we want is someone dying on a bus."

"Thank you so much." I pulled out a bus pamphlet and grabbed a pen off the counter. "Here's my number at work and at home. Call me if you hear anything."

"Sure thing. It's been a while since a pretty woman gave me her number," the clerk said, his hand still on the *Police Gazette*.

Ben frowned. "Thanks for your help. I've got to get this lady back to work."

"Yep, work's a grind, I tell you." The clerk picked up his magazine and stowed it under the counter. We turned and left.

"When you get back to the office, call Milton's wife and find out what's in Denver," Ben said as he opened my car door.

"Gee, I didn't know I worked for the paper."

"You aren't, but I figure she'll talk to you before she talks to me, then give me a call."

Chapter Five

"Denver?" Isabella asked over the phone. I called her from the office upon returning from lunch. "I have no idea. Milton's always talked about how much he wanted to visit Colorado, but he never knew anybody who lived there he would want to visit."

"Well, it sounds like he's on the way there. The bus should arrive at the main terminal in downtown Denver tomorrow. I thought he had a relative there."

"I don't think so. What gets me is where he got the money for a bus ticket. He usually only carries about ten dollars in his wallet at a time. Can you use a Diner's Club charge card for a bus ticket? Jimmy insists he carry one."

"Maybe that's what he used. We issued paychecks on Friday. Could he have cashed that?"

"I guess, but normally he gives me the check. I may have to ask his family to help me pay the bills this month. God knows they won't hurt for it."

Harry Gibson stepped into the office. He was a tall man in his sixties with wisps of gray hair that seemed to grow everywhere, including his ears. The patriarch of the Gibson family was the epitome of a busy man now retired. He wore a tan bomber-style jacket over a brown and gold plaid shirt. The elder Gibson had stepped in to help after Milton's accident. Zipping up his jacket, he approached my desk.

I nodded at him and wrapped up my conversation with Isabella. "I have to go. Keep us posted if you find out anything."

As I hung up, Harry raised an eyebrow. "That my daughter-in-law?"

"Yes. I suppose you've heard about Milton."

Harry scowled at the very mention of his stepson's name. "No. What's he done now? Broken something at the hospital?"

"You don't know? He walked away from the hospital." I was a bit surprised Harry didn't know about Milton's disappearance, but I had just come upon the information myself. It also proved the two families, although joined by marriage, were not close.

Harry's bushy gray eyebrows knitted together for a moment. "Walked away? Are you sure the hospital didn't release him?"

"Very sure, and now he boarded a bus to Denver. Do you have any relatives living in that area?"

Harry shook his head. "I had a cousin up there, but we haven't spoken in years. Milton won't know who that is, the way he forgets things all the time." He put a broad hand over his mouth as if tasting something bad. "You have two sons. A bright-as-a-whip son like Jimmy, and another who stumbles over his own feet like Milton. Which one gives me a grandson? The stumbler. And now it sounds like he's off on some crazy tangent that I'll bet even he doesn't understand."

"Did you ever hear him talk about Denver?"

"Of course not." He glanced at his watch. "Now I have to tell his mother. I have no idea how she's going to take this. She's not been doing well for a while now." Harry turned and walked off.

The radio board squealed behind me. "Calling for Elwood. Is he there?"

I recognized Jimmy's voice and picked up the walkie. "No, he's not. I haven't seen him all day. I figured he was out at the site with you."

"He was for a while, but I can't find him now. Okay. Thanks."

At least he said thanks. Maybe having to do the actual work instead of sitting in his office delegating had softened him.

After that, I made a quick call to the police station to let Mary know about Milton's trip to Denver. Mary shrugged. "It makes no sense to me."

After an hour of absent-minded filing, I was startled by the phone ringing.

"This is the young lady who came into the bus station this morning?" the voice asked without a hello.

"Yes."

"This is Mr. Franklin. Seems we have a situation with your fella."

Had something happened on the bus? Was there another accident? Milton had to be the unluckiest man in America. "Is he okay?"

"Don't rightly know. He got as far as the diner we stop at about an hour out of town. He was on the eleven o'clock bus. Driver says your guy never got back on the bus. Looks like he isn't gonna make it to Denver."

I thanked Mr. Franklin and hung up the phone, then glanced at the clock. I still had forty-five minutes before I could clock out, and an invoice to type up. Milton would have to wait. I picked up the phone and called Mary.

"He left?" she said after I told her about Mr. Franklin's call.

"He got off the bus but never returned."

"We've got to get out to that diner."

"Is Milton an official missing person case yet?"

"Not yet. Isabella thinks he's going to show up. Asked us to wait."

"Are you kidding me?"

"I know, but somehow she feels like this is all a big mistake and that Milton is having some thinking time. If you ask me, she feels guilty about Arturo. I think she has a crush on him. She'll casually mention his name in conversation. You know. Arturo said this or that."

I rolled the invoice into the typewriter, the phone wedged between my ear and my shoulder. "Do you think there was something going on between them?"

"You mean more than friends? They were up to hanky-panky?"

"Yes, if you want to put it that way."

Mary laughed. "I wouldn't think so, but Arturo is a slick customer. He's what they call an ambitious man. If he sees something he wants, he doesn't stop until he gets it."

I began to type, hoping to get the invoice right, while also talking to Mary. "He's very handsome, but he also seems like he knows it."

"Sure, he does. His wife filed for divorce last year because he was cheating on her with Lupe Menendez." I heard a metallic squeak in the background and recognized the familiar sound of Mary's filing cabinet.

"Well, even if he is some kind of Romeo, that doesn't mean he would threaten another man."

"Who knows, but we need to get out to the diner and see if they saw or heard anything unusual. If Isabella won't do it, I will. I'll type up the missing person's report, and the police will start investigating officially tomorrow. Today, though, let's get a jump on things."

"I'll be out of here soon." I glanced at the clock. Five minutes closer. "Forty minutes. Where do you want to meet?"

"Come pick me up after work. The kids are over at their abuela's this afternoon, so I'm free."

This was turning into just the kind of thing Ben loved. "Is it okay if I tell Ben?"

Mary was quiet for a moment. "I don't know. Not yet. Sometimes the press prints things the police need to keep quiet. The last thing we want to do is give out too much information if this is a case of foul play."

"You're right." I hung up the phone and went to work on the invoice, all the while thinking to myself Ben's brain would be good to have in on this.

Chapter Six

"Do you remember this guy?" Mary held up the Camden paper with one of Ben's photos of Milton atop the article about the accident at the demolition site.

The waitress, a woman in her forties with hair that refused to stay pinned up in her light blue sailor cap, squinted. "Yeah, I remember him. The straw king."

There was a couple waiting behind us. "Excuse me," the waitress said. She held up a hand to the couple, gesturing for them to also wait.

"Sure," Mary said. The waitress walked away to an empty table and stacked dirty plates, placing silverware on the top. Mary and I followed her.

"Anything else you remember about him?" Mary asked.

The waitress balanced the plates on the inside of her forearm. "Yeah, he was nervous. We put straws on the tables in these little glass decanters. Not my idea. The boss." She pointed to a tall glass cylinder with a metallic top, then turned her focus to Mary and lowered her voice. "Like he ever worked a day in this joint, wanted to be convenient. Your guy sat there and bent up four straws, like they were toys or something, then left them for us to clean up. The whole time he kept looking out the window."

Now we were getting somewhere. "Do you think he was afraid of someone on the bus?" I looked in the direction of the booth the waitress had glanced at while complaining about the straws.

"How the hell should I know? With a busload of people, I was too busy to keep track of one fidgety guy. When the bus driver came to do his 'all aboard,' the guy had vanished. Stiffed me for the coffee, too. What's wrong

30

with people today?"

Eying the two doors on the opposite wall labeled "Ladies" and "Gents," I asked, "Could he have been in the bathroom?"

"If he was, I sure wasn't checking. I don't make enough in tips to go in there. You never know with some people."

"You bet you don't." Mary walked to the men's room and pushed open the door. "Anyone in here?" After waiting a second, she walked in, and I followed.

I took the first stall, holding my nose from the overwhelming smell of urine. "Look around. Maybe he left a note in one of the stalls. I've heard about people doing that sort of thing."

Men in diners didn't seem to be concerned about flushing, or hitting their target for that matter. I glanced through the various messages written on the wall, adding a few new words to my vocabulary.

The door opened, but Mary stopped some poor man who needed to use the bathroom. "You'll have to hold it, sir. We're doing a police investigation in here. Should be just another minute."

I entered a second stall and began to search around. At the back, where the toilet nestled against the wall, was a wadded-up sheet of paper I instantly recognized. It was a smaller version of one of the blueprints for the demolition.

"Mary, come here."

"You find something?"

I stepped out from the stall to where Mary was standing. "This is from Gibson Construction. Elwood's name is on the top, so it must be his copy." I smoothed out the paper. "Milton had to have been in here. Do you think he just dropped this, or could he have been leaving it for someone to find?"

"Come on, now, Miss Marple. I think you're reaching there. He probably just dropped it."

"Probably. I'd still like to know more. Can I keep it?"

"Seeing as this is a search no one in the police department, besides myself, has authorized, go ahead. Just don't lose it." Another man attempted to enter. "Wait!" Mary shouted. The man stepped back into the restaurant, a little bit of fear in his eyes. Mary turned back to me. "You see anything else?"

"No, just this."

"Good, let's get out of here before my nose is permanently damaged."

When we exited the bathroom, there were three men waiting with various looks of discomfort on their faces.

The waitress came by and noted the small parade rushing into the john. "What's going on back here?"

Mary looked around. "Must be strong coffee. You got a back door?"

"Through the kitchen." We followed her as she carried another stack of dishes behind the counter and through a revolving door. She dropped the dishes into a bus tub and turned around, running straight into my shoulder. "Don't you ladies have something else to do besides bother me? The dinner rush is starting. Move on."

I smiled quickly and nodded. We'd been enough trouble for this lady. "Thanks for your help. We know you're busy."

Mary pulled a dollar bill out of her pocket and handed it to the harried waitress. "Yeah, thanks."

The waitress took the money and deposited it in her bra. "Fab."

"Let's go," Mary said.

As we worked our way through the crowd standing in line for tables, I fidgeted for my keys. Stepping out on the curb, Mary sighed. "He was here, that's for sure."

"Yeah, but then what happened to him?"

"Don't know." The day had turned gray as the sun was setting. In another hour, it would be dark. "What's behind this place?"

I led the way around the building. The diner was a free-standing building facing the road that led to Dallas. Few trees, plenty of scrub brush, and scorched-brown earth. Most diner patrons would be on the road to somewhere else, busses included. The restaurant sat against a large field that backed up to a barbed wire fence.

"Nothing back here," I said.

Mary squinted into the setting sun. "Yeah. It's getting dark, and I need to head back home and make dinner for the kids."

"Well, at least we can tell Isabella we tracked him this far. It all comes back to why he was running."

"And who he was running from," Mary finished. It was amazing to me that all this had just happened, but we had no way of figuring it out.

When I walked into the apartment after the drive home, I found Ellie sitting in front of the black-and-white fifteen-inch RCA with the rabbit ears turned sideways. Her eyes glazed over the gray screen. A pile of hand sewing sat next to her. This time of year, she usually sewed yards of green and red velvet. Her sewing basket often looked like a scene out of a holiday movie. Though Ellie wouldn't admit it, she worked many extra hours after her day at the dress shop doing handwork. She did it every night, and although it was not unusual to see her sitting in front of the television, it was unusual to see her doing nothing. Ellie was a creature always in motion.

I hung my coat up on a hook, my gaze never leaving Ellie's eyes. She wasn't even blinking.

I tried to make my voice sound light, disguising my concern. "Good show?"

Ellie looked up, took a breath, and then gave me a weak smile. "Welcome home. Yeah, I suppose. I wasn't really watching it. Just gathering cobwebs, I guess." Ellie's eyes returned to the television, once again trapped by the latest episode of *The Outer Limits*.

I glanced into the kitchen where Milton's thermos still sat on the counter next to the new phone our landlady, Arlene, had installed for us. She said she was tired of being our receptionist. I was just thankful to have it. "Have you eaten?"

Ellie didn't look away from the screen. Her expression was blank, and the light of the TV flickered off her angled cheekbones. She had thrown her coat over an empty chair. How often had I heard her say, "A place for everything and everything in its place"?

"I'm not hungry." Ellie not being hungry was a sign of end times.

"Not hungry? Are you feeling okay? You're not coming down with something, are you?"

"I'm fine. I just don't feel like eating."

"Ellie. What's going on with you? Is everything okay at the shop?"

She glanced from the TV to the stack of velvet and then frowned. "Everything is great. Better than great. I have too much work. I can barely keep up with it these days."

"Maybe it's time for you to hire an assistant."

Ellie worked solo at her dress shop except for a few temporary hires during wedding season. She always said she couldn't afford the help and couldn't assure the quality of the work if she didn't do it herself. Looking at the stack of unfinished forest green bridesmaids' dresses piled in a heap next to her, maybe her business was outgrowing her management style. Telling Ellie that was another matter altogether.

"I suppose I could hire somebody. It's just I haven't had the energy to talk to anyone since Mrs. Peterson quit to take care of her grandson," Ellie said, no expression on her face.

"That's great. Wouldn't you like to come home and just relax? Not be constantly tying up loose ends from the shop?" Literally.

"Yeah. Great." If I were rating Ellie's enthusiasm on a scale of one to ten, she would currently rate a minus two. I sat next to my cousin and took her hand in mine.

"Okay, what's going on?"

Ellie let out a long, slow breath, as if she had been holding this in for a while. I could tell this was not something she *wanted* to talk about, but what she *needed* to talk about.

"Something's changed. Everything's changed. I don't feel good about life anymore. I know. It's crazy. I used to be the get-up-and-go gal who saw every day as the beginning of a rainbow leading to a pot of happiness. But now? I don't feel that way anymore. I'm tired all the time, not hungry, food doesn't even interest me. If I have one more wishy-washy bride and bossy mother come in, I'm going to lose it." Ellie put her face in her hands. I pulled her into my arms and was even more shocked when she began to sob. "They shot him. They shot him right in the head. His head exploded. How could someone do something like that?"

This had nothing to do with the dress shop. The get-up-and-go and excitement we both had when we got in that taxicab was gone. Ellie had just described my own feelings—how disillusioned I was with my first real job. I felt guilty for not being grateful for this opportunity. I was in a growing business. Camden, being as close as it was to Dallas, was becoming a bedroom community. There would be subdivisions going up to accommodate people who didn't want to live in the city. When I joined Gibson Construction, I thought there would be a career path through this expansion. Instead, my boss was a tyrant, and many of the men I worked around every day didn't respect me. I had landed in a man's world where women were viewed more as servants than coworkers and were the targets of jokes that made me feel uncomfortable. I was working in an office, but my value was somewhere below the new typewriter. I knew what Ellie was feeling. Somehow, the sun wasn't as bright, good wasn't as good, and evil had stepped to the front of the crowd with a smile on his face.

"I've been having the same feelings," I whispered.

"Everything was so good, and now there are people out there with guns waiting in the dark. What's happening to the world?"

For that, I didn't have an answer, and all I could do was cry. After a few minutes, we both sat with our heads leaned back on the couch, exhausted from the outpouring of emotion. The next show had come on, but we barely heard the endless sound of the laugh track droning in the background. Finally, Ellie looked over. "So, how was your day?"

The absurdity of the trivial question after such an emotional release made me laugh. Not a little laugh, but a big one. Ellie laughed, too, letting out a little snort.

"Okay, I guess. Jimmy's brother, Milton, disappeared."

"What? You mean the one that's in the hospital with a head injury? The guy who walked into a wood beam?"

"Same one. Now I guess he's on the lam. From what Mary and I can tell, he disappeared from a diner where the bus he was on stopped. He was going to Denver."

"Denver? What's in Denver?"

"No one really knows."

Ellie slapped me on the knee. "You know, I'm imagining a boogeyman

35

around every corner, but you seem to be actually dealing with one." She stopped and put her hand over her stomach, and a look of surprise came into her eyes. "I'm hungry. You want to go out and get something?"

My heart warmed. "I'd love it."

Chapter Seven

Still holding onto the blueprint from the diner, I knew I needed to find Elwood. The next day I drove over to the demolition site and found him sitting in the excavator, tearing down the last house.

I waved both hands over my head, feeling a little foolish, as I tried to get his attention. Finally, Elwood looked over, a scowl forming on his unshaven face. He shut down the excavator, bucket in midair.

"What?" he barked.

"I need to ask you a question." I walked over to the excavator.

He raised both hands in frustration. "So? I'm in the middle of a demo. Can't it wait?"

"I wouldn't waste your time, but this is important. It has to do with Milton's state of mind before he disappeared." I held up the blueprint. "I found this in the bathroom at a diner where Milton was seen, and it had your name on it." Elwood's lips drew into a line as he put his hands on his knees.

"So? I must have left it somewhere, and Milton picked it up. I don't see how that is important enough to take me off the job." He reached for the key in the ignition.

I stepped closer, feeling my heel sink into the broken ground. "It's important if it's a clue to what was going on with Milton. I'm thinking he left it in the bathroom for a reason."

"Yeah, and maybe he took it out of his pocket to use the john. I've got way too much to do here, so if you're so worked up about it, why don't you ask someone at the bus station or maybe that greasy spoon he was at?"

"We've tried that. Besides, I have to answer the phone at the office."

He shook his head in disgust and reached for the ignition. "Not my problem. But if you want my advice, let the answering machine get the phone. Tell Jimmy you're on company business trying to track down his squirrel-headed brother who ran off in the middle of a project."

As the excavator roared up again, I stepped back. Recalling what had happened to Milton when he got too close to Elwood and that machine, I decided to go back to the diner. Elwood was trying to get rid of me, but at the same time seemed to be giving me permission to go. I rushed back to the office to call the answering service. If Jimmy complained, I could tell him Elwood asked me to go. After that call, I dialed Mary.

"Hey. I can't stop thinking about what Milton left in the bathroom. I'm headed back to the diner. Want to come?"

Mary's file drawer squeaked in the background. "Sure. Let me convince Officer Jerry here that a missing local businessman is more important than filing reports on lost dogs."

"Tell him you need to do something for Isabella. You have a built-in excuse."

When we reached the diner, the sun was glowing through the windows, and the tables were full. The waitress we had spoken to before was not there, but a pleasant, dark-skinned woman holding menus greeted us. "Follow me," she said.

"Oh, we're not here to eat," I assured her. "Were you here when that guy disappeared from the bus?"

The waitress did a slow nod of her head. "Normally, I would say I'm always here, but that day I had to take my daughter to the dentist. I heard a lot about it, though."

"What did you hear?" Mary asked, adopting a conversational tone.

"Just that the guy had some kind of fight outside and then disappeared."

"Did anyone say they saw the person he was fighting with?"

"That's the thing. Everyone saw something different. With that sun, they couldn't even decide if the person was male or female, tall, short, skinny, big. Nothing. What's that they say about every witness seeing a different crime?"

Mary looked impressed. "They do say that. I'm amazed you know that, not being police."

"I read a lot of mysteries. Some days in this place, I feel like committing a homicide, so I read about it instead."

"I get you on that one." Mary walked up to the counter and squeezed between two red stools. "Hey, can we get two pieces of that pie and some coffee?" I gave her a look. "What?" she said. "I'm going to miss lunch by the time we get back."

The pie was apple, and it looked delicious. "We may as well get something out of this trip."

The waitress grinned. "Sure, ladies, and you can call me Claudia. Pretty exciting to have a real live investigation going on at my diner." Claudia led us to an empty table.

After we finished eating our pie—topped with a scoop of ice cream—I ran my fingers over the demolition plan. Why was this important enough for Milton to carry around? If he were escaping something, why would he bring this along? Then leave it in the bathroom. Had he done it on purpose? Or was he leaving this part of his life behind?

"What is that exactly?" Mary asked.

"It's a map of the demolition site, signed by Elwood. The one I found in the bathroom when we were here before. It shows the four houses we are demolishing. I typed the words under the pictures."

Mary took the map from me and turned it around in her hands, squinting at it. She shrugged. "He put it down for a minute and forgot it. No great mystery there."

My gaze strayed to the hand-drawn squares that identified the houses. There was nothing suspicious there. Why would Milton be looking at this right before he disappeared? I noticed a speck—possibly dirt or a stray mark from a number two pencil—in back of the first house. Had he been trying to mark the spot where the beam fell on him?

"You finished?" Mary asked.

"Yes."

"Good, let's check out that field again. Maybe he dropped other things."

"Good idea."

As we crossed the field, empty wrappers and boxes from the diner kitchen littered the short yellow grass. There was something different in the uneven ground before us—something out there, like a big heap of dumped trash. "Do you see that?"

Mary quickened her step. "I sure do."

The sour, rotting smell hit us before we could see what lay on the ground. As we drew closer, I had an involuntary gasp, drawing in a breath of stale air. Milton Gibson, crumpled and bloody, had met his death behind the diner. The side of his face was bloodied, and one eye dangled where his skull had caved in under the new bandage. So soon after seeing Kennedy's head, this sight hit me like a freight train, and I felt my knees buckle. This couldn't be happening again.

When the police arrived, they pushed me away from the scene to the parking lot. Mary, even though she was a uniformed policewoman, was told to guard the scene.

"But sir, I have some essential information about this death," Mary told the male officer. At five feet, two inches, she looked childlike next to the officer who towered over her by a foot. He nodded and gave her a condescending smile. "I'm sure you have lots to tell me, and you think it's important, but let us investigate the crime scene with our trained eyes. We'll get to you later." He looked at another male officer with a grin and a wink.

Mary lifted her jaw. "With all due respect, sir, I went to the same police academy you did, and I can investigate a crime scene."

"Yeah, well," he put a hand to his chin, cocking his head to the side. "Just because they let you in doesn't make you a cop. Stand guard on the perimeter, and that's an order. Comprende?"

"Yes, sir," Mary answered with a crisp edge to her voice. "The victim is also my brother-in-law, sir. With your permission, I would like to inform the family."

Where many policemen at this point might soften a little, Mary's superior stayed unmoved. "I see. Well, you need to stay posted until I can get someone else out here to take your place." He clipped an obligatory "Sorry for your loss." Without another word, he turned back to the body in the field.

Ben drove up in his dilapidated Chevy, kicking up gravel as he came to a stop. He leaned over the passenger seat for his camera and notepad and then jumped out. "You found Milton?"

"About an hour ago." I pointed a finger backwards over my shoulder.

"What happened to him?" Ben moved closer, but Mary stepped forward, feet spread and hands behind her back.

"Stop right there. It's a crime scene. No press."

"We have to be fifty yards back," he complained, his lanky arm gesturing toward the crime scene. "Can't you let me get a little closer? I can't get a clear shot from here." He lifted his camera slightly.

Mary brought her hands to the front and crossed her arms. "Then take a picture of the diner."

Ben put down the camera and took out the small notepad. "How about the two of you tell me what you found? Did you get a statement from Isabella? How is she doing right now? What did it look like when you walked up to the dead body of Milton Gibson?"

Mary rolled her eyes. "No comment."

"I'll tell you," I said as Mary's gaze darted to me. "Not everything, Mary. Just an overall impression." I turned back to Ben. "It was awful. We couldn't get away from there fast enough. Trust me, you don't want a picture of Milton the way he looks now. It's better to remember him the way he was."

Ben nodded. "You're right. The newspaper wouldn't print anything too gory, anyway." Mary looked relieved, so I continued. "Also, even though Mary was the first officer on the scene, they have assigned her to the parking lot because she's a woman."

Ben looked confused. "That's her job, isn't it?"

"No." My hands went up in the air in frustration. "Her job is to investigate crime. She's not some glorified security guard."

"Please, Dot. It's my battle. You don't have to fight it." Mary looked a little embarrassed. "I don't want the entire world knowing."

"But what's the use of going through the academy if they won't let you use what you were taught? It's ridiculous."

Ben jumped in. "You know, this might make a human-interest story. We could profile what it's like to be a woman in a man's world, and you're from—" He bit his bottom lip. "Mexico?"

"I'm an American, like you, and I do not want to be the subject of your article. Take a picture of the diner and wait for the department to make a report on the death. Okay?"

"Sure, if that's the way you want it."

Within the hour, the investigating officers returned to the curb, putting away notepads.

The officer that had assigned Mary to the curb walked up with his arms crossed. "Okay, Officer Oliva. We've checked out the body. Victim of blunt force. Someone sure made a dent in his skull. What did you want to add?"

Mary took out her own pocket notepad, but unlike Ben's, this one was police issue. "I made a few notes, sir. Mr. Gibson previously sustained a head injury from falling debris at a construction site. He walked away in the middle of a hospital stay. Many witnesses noted he seemed nervous about something. He boarded a bus for Denver, although no one knows who he would visit there. He only made it as far as this diner."

"Could be useful," the officer interrupted. "Uh, type it up and put it on my desk."

"But there's more."

"I'm sure there is." Without another word or even a thank you, he walked to his car.

I watched him stride away. "Do they always talk to you like that?"

"Nope. Sometimes it's worse."

Another police car pulled up, and two young men, looking fresh out of the academy, joined us. The thinner one of the two addressed Mary. "We're here to relieve you, sir. We heard you're related to the vic."

"Yes, thank you."

"It's rotten you had to be the one to find him. Can we do anything else for you?" Here was a policeman with a heart. I had to wonder if he would someday be as callous and cold as the commanding officer at this crime scene. Is that what happens after years of seeing the worst in people?

"No," Mary gulped as her eyes filled. "And thank you." She looked at me.

"This is going to be hard on Isabella. It's just hitting me."

"Let's get to the car." I put my arm around Mary's shoulders as she began to shake. As long as she'd been on the job, she held it together, but now the impact of it all was getting to her.

The parking lot of Sunny Side Diner was filling up as a red pickup pulled into the space next to my car. Jimmy Gibson hit the pavement looking like an angry bear. Spotting me, he strode over, purpose in his step. "What happened?"

His tone made me feel like I was guilty of something. "He's back there. I'm so sorry."

Jimmy shoved his hands in his pockets, paced a few steps, and then said, "I have to see him." Mary stopped him, but he pulled away. The other officers then stood in front, blocking his access to the crime scene.

"I need to see my brother."

"You don't want to do that, sir. Let the police do their jobs."

Jimmy tried one more push forward but then gave up. He closed his eyes and dropped his head for a moment, but then looked up at me. "Oh, God. I need to tell our parents. This is going to kill them."

For the first time, I saw my boss softening in front of me. From the first day of my employment, he'd been abrupt, rude, and hard to please. Now his human side seemed to be slipping out like a shy child. "I never should have spoken to him the way I did. I should have been kinder to Milton." He put a hand to his face, and his shoulders heaved. "I just heard about it when someone came to the site. They'd heard it on the radio. I was there all afternoon. Thank goodness my mother watches her stories on weekdays. She won't know anything about it yet, I hope. "

"Why don't you take a seat in your truck, sir? Pull yourself together." I put a hand under his elbow and gently guided him back to his vehicle. "Would you like me to get you some water? Or we could go into the diner for a cup of coffee?"

Jimmy opened his truck door. On the seat was a bag with a hamburger logo on the front. I could smell the fries. He looked toward the diner. "No. I'd rather stay out here."

"Of course. Do you have any idea who would want to do this to him? He was frightened of something or someone. Did he tell you anything?"

"Frightened? What would frighten him?" His tone was quickly returning to the old Jimmy. He knitted his bushy eyebrows together as he thought. "Milton never told me he was frightened. Maybe it was the concussion that confused him. He wasn't right in the head, you know? I wish I would have seen it in him. I could have helped. It's hell to think your brother's last memory of you was bad." He put his head in his hands again and cried.

I looked over at Mary, whose face had gone pale. She had to be thinking of the sad job of telling her own family. One man dies, and it affects so many people.

Chapter Eight

After taking a few minutes to collect himself, Jimmy announced he would go back to the office and call his father. From there, the family could get together and plan Milton's funeral. For some reason, Jimmy never asked why I wasn't at work, so I didn't provide any details. I followed him in my car back to the office as Mary went to comfort her sister-in-law.

When Jimmy unlocked the door, Elwood darted up from behind Jimmy's desk. He was out of breath, as if getting caught with his hand in a cookie jar. "Hey, boss. Didn't expect to see you. Lost my darn lighter. I guess I'll have to buy a new one."

"Why was the door locked?" Jimmy asked.

Elwood nervously rubbed his right hand on his leg. "Don't know."

"I'm sure you've heard the news," Jimmy said.

Seeming to change gears, Elwood casually walked to the front of the desk as the two men switched places. "Yeah. Sorry. Do they know who did it?" I hadn't noticed before, but Elwood held a folded piece of paper in his left hand. He slid it into the pocket of his dark gray denims.

Jimmy banged his knee on an open drawer Elwood had just maneuvered around. Had Elwood been searching through the desk drawers? "Dammit, Milton. That boy can't close a drawer or a cabinet to save himself."

"What a loser," Elwood quickly agreed and nodded but then stopped himself. This was a familiar pattern between the two men. But now that Milton was dead, they could no longer blame all the ills of the world on Milton. Elwood stuttered. "I mean, do they know who did it?"

"They barely know how it was done, let alone who." Jimmy placed his finger on the dial of his black desk phone when he looked back at Elwood. "Did you need something else?"

"Uh, no. My condolences, boss." Elwood cleared his throat.

"Yeah, well, skedaddle. I have to call my parents. I should probably do this in person, but at least this way, it spares me some of the theatrics." He looked over at me. "And you. I won't need you anymore today. We'll finish up our submission for the Golden Hammer tomorrow. I'd like some privacy."

"Sure," I said, silently cheering my early dismissal. "Let me know if there's anything you need."

"Will we be working tomorrow?" Elwood asked.

"No. We'll lose a day on the project. Tell the men to take the rest of the day off."

"Only one day?"

"We aren't giving out free vacation days, you know. Now, if you don't mind." Jimmy shooed them out with his hand. I followed Elwood out the door.

Once outside, Elwood took a lighter and a pack of cigarettes out of his pocket. "Thought we'd at least be off until the funeral. Ol' Milton screws up everything, even dying." He lit his cigarette and took a long draw, smoke exiting his nostrils.

"I guess time is money, especially if you're Mr. Gibson."

"If you're Jimmy, everything is money. That's the way he thinks. If he had it his way, he'd have us working morning, noon, and night. I've worked harder for him than anyone else in town." Elwood's hand strayed to his pocket. Whatever he grabbed, he was now tracing the outline with his finger.

"Hey, I thought you lost your lighter?"

Elwood looked at the lighter in his hand as if it had magically appeared. "I have an extra, so what?"

"That's pretty convenient, carrying around two lighters. You must lose a lot of lighters. You know, I saw you fold something and put it in your pocket."

Elwood pulled the cigarette from his mouth and glared at me. Whatever was in his pocket, he didn't look happy I'd brought it up.

"What are you? The office police? It was a work schedule, so mind your own business. I don't tell you how to do your job."

"I just find it all strange. You lost your lighter. You have a lighter. You need paperwork, but then you hide it in your pocket."

"Like I said, none of your business, and if you know what's good for you, you'll stop asking stupid questions. It was bad enough when Milton was around. The last thing we need is for you to start up." Elwood stepped closer to me, making me feel surrounded by his large frame. "You're not bad to look at, but I prefer you not talking a whole hell of a lot. Women are better that way."

What a jerk. I stepped back and slung my purse strap over my shoulder. "I prefer you the same way—silent, or better yet—gone." I marched to my car, hoping I'd gotten away with my exit line. I was also sure that whatever Elwood had put into his pocket was not a work schedule. He'd been digging around Jimmy's desk, and whatever he found, he didn't want anyone else to know about it. Had this to do with Milton's death? One thing was for sure. I would never be alone with Elwood again if I could help it. At least until I figured out if he was safe. After Milton's death, I didn't trust him.

The phone was ringing as I stepped into my apartment. I pulled off a clip earring and kicked off my heels as I placed the receiver to my ear.

"Dot, what's this I'm hearing about you finding a body?" The familiar sound of a stamp clicking onto paper echoed in my ear. My mother was at the checkout desk at the library, giving someone two weeks to explore the world in a book.

"It was Milton from work. You know, the boss's brother?"

Slightly away from the phone, she said, "Thank you very much. Be sure to return them on time." Then the volume of her voice filled out as she brought her mouth closer to the mouthpiece. "You mean the man who got hit by a piece of wood at the demolition a few days ago?"

"Yes." I filled my mother in on the details, leaving out some of the gory parts.

"Amazing. This must be one of those instances when, if it's your time, it's your time. I guess it was Milton's time. Is there anything we can do for the family?"

There was a knock at the door. "Uh, Mom. Someone's here. I'll let you know."

Hanging up, I put my heels back on and, upon opening the door, found Ben standing with a bag of sandwiches from Colombo's. "I thought after all we've seen today, you might need a delicious dinner to share with your favorite professional journalist." I looked down the stairs to see Arlene smiling and waving at the bottom.

"Come on in. I'm surprised Arlene is okay with you coming upstairs." This was an unexpected and most welcome surprise. I led him to the couch, where he placed the bag on the coffee table.

"Why wouldn't she be? After all, I was a Boy Scout. So, did you learn anything else after I left?"

I shook my head. "You sure don't waste any time. I thought you were here for me, but it seems you're here for the story."

"Am I that obvious?"

"Like an army recruiter at a high school graduation."

Ben opened the bag, pulling out sandwiches wrapped in white deli paper, and handed one to me. "It isn't all my pursuit of the news, you know. Maybe I'm in pursuit of you."

I could feel the heat rising in my cheeks. We had been seeing each other off and on, but I still wasn't sure if we were a budding romance, or two friends enjoying each other's company. "That's some smooth talking."

He gave a lopsided grin, causing a dimple to come out on one cheek. He was charming. There was no doubt about it. Why was it that when I looked at him, I saw the picket fence, the two kids, the Oldsmobile? All of it. A month ago, I would have happily continued feeling that way, but as hard as I tried, something in me was changing. I now knew I would never be Doris Day, and he would never be Rock Hudson. Especially now that people were bringing guns to parades.

"Not much happened. Jimmy came out to the scene, and he was full of regret for being so mean to his brother."

"Too late now."

"Don't I know it? I followed him back to the office, where he was going to call his parents. I can't think of a tougher thing to do."

"I'll bet the police appreciated it."

"Yeah, but when we walked in, we found Elwood, the foreman, under Jimmy's desk. He looked...I don't know, guilty."

Ben took a big bite and then seemed to swallow it whole. "What do you think he was doing?"

"I have no idea, but he had something he was trying to stash in his pocket. A piece of paper."

Ben leaned back on the couch. "Hmm. Wonder what old Elwood is trying to keep secret?"

"I wish I knew. Jimmy's only giving the crew today off and the afternoon the day of the funeral."

"He's all heart."

"I think that family only had one heart between three men, and the one who got it was Milton."

"You mean the father is like Jimmy?" He grabbed at a French fry.

"He seems to be. He probably wouldn't give the crew any more time off. Harry had a favorite son and didn't mind if the other one knew it. Remember, Milton was his stepson. I can't tell you how many times since I've been there that Harry has complained about Milton slowing things down."

"Enough to kill him?"

I took a bite of my sandwich and thought for a moment. Could Harry really kill his son? He was a stepson, but still, he'd raised him. It took a cold heart to do something like that. "Don't know."

"What was Milton doing to slow things down?"

"He was late going down to the city office to get the permits. That was one." I searched my memory. "Oh, and he didn't have the replacement parts for the excavator. They had to wait a day for that. It was always minor stuff."

Ben crumpled up the paper from his sandwich. "Doesn't seem like a reason to kill a man, but it is almost impossible to fire a family member."

"After working for the Gibsons, I can tell you they're hotheads. I'm sure

Jimmy's blood pressure has to be through the roof."

"Yeah, nobody said being the boss is easy." He rose from the couch. "I'd better get going."

"Where are you off to in such a hurry?"

"I feel like paying a call on Elwood Kirk. Get his up close and personal view of all that's going on. Let him know how much I value his opinion."

"Yeah, well, you better make sure he knows it might end up in print."

"Madam." Ben put the back of his hand to his forehead. "You offend me. I would never print anything without getting permission first."

"Thank you for dinner."

"My pleasure." Ben leaned down to where I was sitting on the couch. I felt my breath shorten as his lips neared mine. There was a warm twinkle in his eyes, and that damn dimple appeared again as a smile played on his lips. He raised up an inch or two and kissed me on the forehead. It was like going to the cliff to see the glorious seashore and then falling off. He squeezed my shoulder and left.

Feeling a little down, I decided to take a hot bath, partly to soak away my troubles and partly to think. Just as I was starting to size up the clues, suspects, and motives, the phone rang. I jumped out of the tub, grabbed a robe, and bounded across the small apartment to the kitchen. At first, there was no sound on the other end, and then a deep breath filled the earpiece. A low guttural voice edged out, "You'd better mind your own business, Dot. Sending the press to me was not a good idea."

"Elwood?" I couldn't be sure because whoever it was sounded drunk.

"You know, accidents happen all the time. Just ask Milton. Oh, sorry, guess you can't. If you do anything else to interfere and stick that pretty nose in where it doesn't belong, I'll make sure you never butt in again. Tell me you get the message."

"Who is this?"

"You and your cousin have a real nice apartment on the second floor of that old biddy's house, but I should tell you, it might be a good idea to pull the shades."

The apartment had one window that let in perfect light in the afternoons.

From now on, I would keep the shade pulled down. "I get your message. Who is this?"

There was a click on the other end. Ellie came to the kitchen and put the teakettle on. "Who was that?"

"I don't know. It might have been Elwood Kirk, but I'm not sure. Whoever it was, he was drunk."

Ellie nodded. "Oh, one of those calls. I hate those things. What did he say?"

"That I should butt out of trying to figure out who killed Milton. It had to be Elwood because he mentioned sending the press to him. Ben said he was going to interview him for the paper. I have to call Ben."

Not feeling like getting back in a cold tub, I put on pajamas and dialed the number I kept on a piece of paper next to the phone. If Ben found Elwood, he didn't waste any time. "Did you interview Elwood tonight?"

"I did. I also ran into Harry Gibson and talked to him. He and Elwood were having a drink together. Why?"

I considered what I would say next. If I told Ben I received a threatening call, he might suggest that I step back from the investigation. Mary would say the same. "I was curious. What did he have to say?"

"Dot Morgan. I think you just made up an excuse to call me. You know, even though my mother would never approve, it's okay for a woman to call a man. In fact, it's very modern of you."

"Don't let it go to your head. What did he say?"

"He told me to mind my business. Both did. I don't plan to follow their suggestion. The more they clam up, the more there is to find. So, now, what else do you want to talk about?" His tone had changed to playful. But after my prior phone call, I wasn't in the mood.

"Nothing. I need to go. See you tomorrow?"

"You can count on it."

Chapter Nine

"Dang it!" Another mistake. I'd been making mistakes all morning, and my typewriter eraser was getting too dirty to erase cleanly. It's one thing to make a mistake on one piece of paper, but I was typing in triplicate with two carbons inserted between the three pages of typing paper. So, one mistake equaled three. I rubbed at the error with my eraser, leaving a black streak. I felt my heart sink and my frustration rise as I realized I would have to start over.

Glancing out the window, I scanned the parking lot. I'd been watching for Elwood all morning, hoping to avoid him. Milton was the only one at Gibson Construction who had treated me like an equal. He was the only positive thing in an office of gloom and doom.

I hadn't seen Jimmy yet, but Harry called in to tell me the family would depend on me to hold down the fort while they made final preparations for Milton.

"I'd be happy to do all I can, Mr. Gibson."

Harry cleared his throat. "Thank you. We can't bury him yet because of the ongoing investigation, but we're going to have a memorial at St. Catherine's. Jimmy's handling the details."

"How is he doing?"

"He's forging ahead. It's all we can do in times like these. Milton had his troubles, but family is family even if he isn't blood."

I heard the door of the office open, and I dreaded looking up. Was Elwood finally coming to fulfill his threat?

"Dot. I need you to make a few phone calls for me." It was Jimmy. He slid a piece of paper onto my desk. "Here's Milton's obituary. Call it into the paper and then type up a copy to distribute to the printer. I've just come from the mortuary. We have a casket once we get the body back from the police."

I glanced at the obituary and then at Jimmy. Here he was, handing me his brother's handwritten obituary, and it didn't feel any different than when he pushed a purchase order across my desk. When my grandmother died, I had dark circles under my eyes from crying, and Jimmy had been shaken when he first showed up at the diner. But now he looked fine. Energized, even. Maybe men reacted differently to grief than women, I thought. "Did you write this?"

"My stepmother did."

There were a few streaks where the ink looked like moisture had hit it. He might not be crying, but chances were his mother did when she wrote the obituary. After all, Milton was her biological son. "Any progress with the investigation?"

"No. They've been talking to people on the bus and in the diner. One waitress said he was arguing with some guy outside. They were trying to match the description with a bus passenger, but nothing. The bus was parked to the side with the sun hitting off it. The glare blocked their view. I doubt they could see anything."

Who had Milton been arguing with? Had Elwood Kirk come after him to finish the job he had started at the demolition? It hardly seemed like a reason to murder him. I had to know. "You were around Milton and Elwood more than I was. How bad was it between them?"

Jimmy scowled and gave me a cockeyed look. "Why do you care?" I recognized that scowl because he used to look at Milton the same way when he'd made a mistake.

"Aren't you in the least bit curious why Elwood was crawling under your desk yesterday?"

Jimmy rubbed the back of his neck. "He said he dropped something."

"I don't think he did. He was getting something from your desk. Could you check and see if anything is missing?"

"Are you sure it wasn't you who got hit on the head out there? Elwood

Kirk is the best hire I've made in years. Not only is he a great foreman, but he helps me keep all those knuckleheads I hire in line. Whatever he was doing under my desk was his own damn business. He runs a tight ship and turns in his paperwork on time. It's what I like about him. You're barking up the wrong tree. If you're going to go after somebody, go after Arturo Galvez. The wife's boyfriend is the most likely suspect. Don't you think?"

"I didn't know you heard about Arturo, but I don't think he's her boyfriend. She's married. Do you know him?"

He pointed a stubby finger at me. "Camden isn't that big, of course, I know him. It's hard to keep secrets around here. Now, if you could get the obituary done in the next few hours, and quit worrying about our foreman, you might get to keep this job."

After Jimmy left, I went to work on the obituary. Out of habit, I typed it in triplicate. Just as I got to listing Milton's family members, I made a mistake. Would this day ever end? When I finally finished with my typing, I decided to call Mary at the precinct. "How's Isabella?"

"As good as she can be, I guess. Their marriage wasn't perfect. Even so, it's extremely hard on her. I think the person you really should be concerned about is John. He's torn up. Milton was more than his brother-in-law. He was an army buddy. It's hard to beat a bond like that once you've been through all the stuff soldiers go through."

"What do you know about Arturo Galvez? Could he have been threatening Milton?"

"Why would he do that?"

"This is just what I heard. I'm not sure if it's true, but I heard he had an interest in Isabella, and maybe, just maybe, she had an interest in him."

Mary didn't answer at first and then lowered her voice. "I was wondering."

"What do you mean?"

"I can't be sure. It's only my observation, and I might be blowing it all out of proportion, but at her birthday party last month, I noticed Isabella and Arturo off to the side. They were talking, and well, she kept smiling. If I didn't know she was married to Milton, I would have said they were flirting with each other."

I stacked my work on the desk. "Interesting. What kind of guy is Arturo?"

"He can be a hothead. No doubt about it. He runs a service company. His company offers foundation repair and exterminator services as well as plumbing and electric services. He's been an enormous success and has a lot of men on the payroll. Surely you've seen those AG Services trucks around town. Seems like there's more of them every week. I have heard some people complaining that it's killing the little guys in Camden, though. I heard the commercial on the radio. Sink stopped up and lights went out, just call CA9-7777 and give us a shout!"

I knew one of those little guys. Ellie's fiancé, Al Maxwell, was a self-employed electrician. How much had AG Services cut into his business? If Arturo got whatever he wanted, then how far would he go to get Isabella away from Milton? "Have the police questioned him?"

"Yes. They brought him in because he was one of the people who spoke to Milton in the last week. Unfortunately, it was Officer Jerry who questioned him, and I think they both spent the time comparing how far they could puff out their chests. Men."

"Where does it put him on the suspect list?"

"He's at the bottom. No, they're going with the drifter angle, either on the bus or in the diner."

"What about the man he was arguing with outside the restaurant?"

"We asked people in the diner and the bus to describe the guy, but the sun was obviously an issue. We have a short, tall, white, Mexican, black, heavy-set, athletic man. Eyewitnesses can be about as reliable as a fortune cookie."

Chapter Ten

The next day, work continued on the demolition, and I stopped after work to check in on Mary and John on the way to my parents' house. They were having a special dinner with my grandmother, who was visiting from Waco. She liked to have Christmas at her house, so years ago, my parents settled on having her visit the first week of December.

Before that, I was hoping to talk to Isabella and learn more about her relationship with Arturo. She and Freddie had been staying with Mary and John since Milton's death, but Isabella had to be thinking about returning home. This might be a good time to have free access to her. The more I learned about Milton's life, the more I felt sorry for him. His family didn't like him. His own brother belittled him, and now his wife might have been cheating on him. Yet every day, he came to the office with a smile on his face. The person who can live in such a hostile environment and still cheer others is a rarity. I knew I would do everything I could to get justice for this man.

"Dot? We didn't expect you." Mary opened the door and invited me in. Isabella sat on the couch, a colorful crocheted throw over her.

"Hi, Isabella. How are you doing?" Isabella didn't look at me even though I had asked her a question. I took a chair next to the couch.

"How do you think I'm doing? Someone murdered my husband."

"Isabella." John spoke through the breakfast bar between the kitchen and living room. "She was only asking. You don't need to be rude."

Isabella looked indifferent to her brother's scolding. "I'm fine. Just fine. In fact, I think I'll go out for ice cream later to round out this perfect day."

"I'm sorry," I said. Maybe this hadn't been a good idea. Even if she had been cheating on Milton, she was obviously grieving. "I've come at a bad time. If you need anything, let me know."

"I don't need anything." Her answer was flat and dismissive.

Mary motioned for me to move to the door. We stepped outside, away from Isabella. "She's been like that all day today. No matter what I try to do, she snarls at me. I'll be glad when all this is over. I guess I should be thankful Milton's family has taken over the funeral preparations."

"Memorial," I corrected.

"Memorial. Hopefully, the coroner's office will finish with him soon. We expect the burial to be sometime next week. Isabella has been talking about suing Gibson Construction because of Milton's accident. John said Arturo came by while I was at work, and the two of them had their heads together."

If Isabella sued the Gibsons, she might have a case. Elwood Kirk bullied Milton, and the beam hitting Milton could have been an accident—one of those things—or someone could have been trying to kill him. As I recalled that day, I remembered the thermos.

"Hey, I still have Milton's thermos. I should have brought it by today. I picked it up the day he was hit."

A smirk came across Mary's face. "I doubt she cares what happens to that thermos. You might as well throw it away."

"I would think she'd want it. He loved it because it was a gift from her."

"Think what you want, but I know Isabella."

An hour later, I was at my parents' house telling my mother about Isabella as she mashed potatoes. "Do you think she could have been cheating on Milton? He was so nice. It's hard to believe."

"Yeah, well, it happens, Pumpkin." The nickname my father used was sweet and endearing, but I hoped he wouldn't call me that where anyone else could hear.

"It never happened to the two of you," I said.

My parents exchanged a look, and I repeated my question. "It didn't, did it?"

"Of course not," my mother said.

"Although your mother did have a library patron who fancied her for a while. He would only check out his books with her."

Mother reached out and gave Dad a loving push. "Stop. The man was ninety-three."

"There might be snow on the roof, but—"

"Stop." That was the way my parents were. Even after thirty years of marriage, they were still playful. I hoped someday I would still have that with my husband, whoever he was.

"Opal, you need any help?" My grandmother called out from the next room. She never trusted her daughter to meet her demanding standards.

"Thank God you made her wait at the table. Her yearly visits get longer and longer," Mother whispered to my father.

He raised his eyebrows and smiled warmly. "I thought you might need a little less stress."

To my surprise, she kissed my father on the cheek. "I only wish you would've told her years ago, dear."

"All for my love." My father headed to the dining room, arms full of mashed potatoes and cornbread stuffing.

I fingered the heart at my neck. Something about this delicately crafted piece of jewelry made me want to wear it. Perhaps it was the mystery surrounding it. Who had been the original owner? Was it a gift from someone she loved? When did she lose it? It could have been a treasure passed down for generations.

"What a lovely necklace," my mother said. "Where did you get it?"

"Milton found it at the demolition site. Once I cleaned it up, I started wearing. Didn't it come out nice?"

"It sure did." She moved closer and took the delicate heart in her hand. "You can see the fine lines of engraving."

Mother took a moment longer. "Just beautiful, but I'd better get a move on. Your grandmother doesn't like to wait too long." She took gravy off the stove and poured it into a bowl. "Irma Jean Bagley told me she saw you and Ben Dalton at the lunch counter this week."

I felt the heat rising to my cheeks, no doubt turning a shade of pink. "Yes, he's been helping me figure out all this stuff going on with Gibson

Construction."

She gave me a wry smile. "I'll bet he is. Don't forget, he is a reporter."

"He's my friend. He's not in it for the story." At least, I hoped so. It would break my heart if he only pretended to be interested in me to get a scoop on Milton's murder. When I thought of those blue eyes and ready grin, there wasn't any way he couldn't be sincere. "Trust me, Mom. I know what I'm doing."

"I think he's a genuinely nice young man. Anyone who makes his living with the written word is okay in my book."

"So says the librarian," I laughed.

"Well, does he have any theories about who killed Milton?"

"No, but the police need to look at Elwood Kirk."

She raised an eyebrow as she added a serving spoon to the bowl. "The foreman? Why would he want to hurt Milton?"

"He's hiding something, for sure."

Later, as I gathered my things to leave, my mother placed a gentle hand on my arm. "If you think something is amiss, then go through everything Elwood has touched. You might come up with something."

I nodded. "First chance I get."

Chapter Eleven

The next day, all the houses at the demolition site were finally down, and trucks were hauling away the debris. Although the memorial service was in a few hours, Jimmy Gibson was focused on the next phase of the project. He sat at his cluttered desk, looking at the file for the strip mall project. "Where are the permits?"

I sifted through the strewn paperwork to find the permits and placed them on the top of the pile. After that, I returned to typing up a bid for a job after the strip center project. Jimmy had plans to develop more commercial property in Camden, and his next move was to bid on a vacant lot with an abandoned liquor store next to it.

Jimmy shuffled through the stack. "Where's the electrical permit? Didn't we apply for this? Good God, that Milton."

When Jimmy was in the throes of business, his true feelings about his brother came to light. Jimmy was like his father, where Milton had been more the sensitive type. Sometimes Milton reminded me of the Charlie Brown character from the funny pages in the newspaper. He tried to succeed, but Jimmy, the proverbial Lucy, would pull the football out from under him every time.

"It should be in there," I said.

"Well, it isn't. What do I pay you for if you can't keep important files straight?" he grumbled.

I searched my memory, trying to remember anything about the permit. Electric, concrete, mechanical. Had I lost the electric permit? I couldn't be sure.

"And where is the roster of the men's hours so far on the project? That's gone, too. How am I supposed to plan a budget without that?"

"Sir, I don't know where these documents are, but I'll spend the rest of my day searching for them if I have to."

Jimmy shook his head in disgust. "You know, all I have to do is call up that secretarial school, and I can have another girl here in a moment. I thought you were the best they had to offer."

My heart raced. It was one thing to quit my job after only a month, but to get fired would be much worse. The phone rang, interrupting my thoughts.

"I need to talk to you." Ellie was on the other end, and from the tone of her voice, she wasn't doing well.

"What's wrong?"

Jimmy looked over. "Is this a private phone call during business hours?"

I chose to ignore him as I listened to my cousin. I could hear the urgency in her voice.

"It's Al."

"Did something happen to Al?"

"No. Not exactly. I need to talk to you."

I glanced at Jimmy. If I didn't get off the phone in the next ten seconds, he'd call the secretarial school for another "girl." However, I wasn't sure who I was saving, me or the next secretary.

"Can we talk at lunch? This is an inconvenient time. I'm working."

Ellie drew out a long-exasperated sigh. "Lunch? My life is on edge, and I have to wait until you get a bowl of soup?"

"Please." I tried for a forceful undertone.

"Fine. Meet me at the lunch counter at twelve." Ellie hung up.

"Sorry about that." I replaced the phone in the receiver. "It was my cousin. She's having a bit of an emergency."

"You said, Al." Jimmy looked more interested than perturbed. That was a relief. "Is that Al Maxwell, the electrician?"

"Yes, he is."

"He bid on the strip mall project."

"Did he?" I hadn't seen all the bids that had come in because Jimmy preferred to go out and ask certain contractors.

"Yeah. A verbal bid. He was one of four companies, but in the running. Something happened to him?"

"Not a clue, but I'm meeting my cousin for lunch. Al is her boyfriend."

"I hate to bow to the prices over at AG Services, but Galvez has so many guys working for him. That S. O. B. is going to be running this place before long. Guys like Al may not be around for long. It's too bad AG Services is undercutting the little guy, but price is a big deal for us contractors."

Jimmy had no idea how close he might be to the truth. And if Arturo married Isabella, he'd have a direct tie to Jimmy's most prized possession, Gibson Construction. Had Jimmy thought of this? He probably didn't even know about Arturo and Isabella having an affair.

When I met Ellie for lunch, she had surprising news.

"Al has decided the engagement is over, and he wants to run away to Las Vegas to get married." Ellie slurped at the straw of her soda rapidly, the drink, long gone.

"How do you feel about that?"

Ellie made stunning bridal ensembles. I had a tough time believing she'd even consider anything other than a traditional wedding.

"Paul Newman and Joanne Woodward did it. So did Steve Lawrence and Eydie Gormè, but we're not that kind of people. We're not glamorous or flashy. It's like something's put a fire under him, and he can't wait. I thought we were going to have a June wedding. I've always dreamed of being a June bride, but he says I'm way too busy that month sewing dresses for all the other June brides." She put her face in her hands. "I don't know what to do."

I put an arm around my cousin. "But this is what you want, isn't it?"

"Yes. I don't know. Dot, ever since Dallas, things are different. I don't feel the same about anything, including Al."

"You mean you don't think you want to marry him anymore?"

"Well, it isn't like we were waiting to, you know. You know, to...I feel rushed. We were so damn happy, you know? A month ago, I'd have been painting 'Vegas or Bust' on the back of Al's truck, but now the world has changed."

I knew exactly what Ellie was saying. The world had changed. It was hard to think about happily ever after when it could be taken away so quickly.

Chapter Twelve

Milton's memorial was a quiet and somber affair, particularly when compared to the last few turbulent days of his life. The priest talked about how Milton was a valuable part of Gibson Construction, a loyal son, and a loving husband. Too bad the people who received those gifts of value, loyalty, and love didn't appreciate them. Following the service, the crowd moved from the funeral home to a small get-together at Milton's parents' house. I attended alone because Ellie was in no mood to go to the memorial, but Mary told me she would try to make an appearance. She continued to hit resistance from her fellow officers to have a part in the investigation, but that didn't mean she was spending all her time filing. I was keeping her up to date on everything I discovered, and Mary was doing the same for me. Mary had permission to attend the memorial because Milton was family, but other than that, her superior officers took little notice of her.

I grabbed a plate and put a small piece of cake on it, but I was still full from lunch. Other guests were choosing from fried chicken, potato salad, ham and field peas, and collard greens. Classic Texas funeral fare. The Gibsons' house was large, with a lot of beautiful built-ins, including china cabinets and bookshelves. As I walked around, I noticed Harry's home office, a study off the front parlor. He had a world map tacked up on the wall and a hurricane map placed in a glassed-in wooden frame. There was a grease pencil tied to a string hanging off a nail on the side. That must be where he tracked the hurricanes using the radio broadcasts. My father would spread a map out on the table to keep track. Nothing as fancy as the Gibson set up, but when there was a swirling cloud in the Gulf, keeping on top of radio updates was crucial. The padded leather office chair that had been facing the window suddenly began to turn. Little Freddie Gibson sat in the chair, holding tight to a small brown teddy bear. I couldn't blame him. I couldn't imagine being so young and expected to endure his father's memorial, just like the adult members of his family.

"Hi, Freddie. Did you have something to eat? Lots of great food out there."

The little boy's face was pale. "I'm not hungry."

"Why are you in here all by yourself?"

"I don't know."

I could have kicked myself for asking such a stupid question when the answer was obvious—he'd been looking for a quiet place to hide. I tried to make it better. "You know what? I really liked working with your dad. Sometimes when your Uncle Jimmy would get angry with me, your dad told me to hang on and smile. It made Jimmy nervous. I tried it once, and it worked."

A little color came into Freddie's cheeks. "He did? He told you that?"

"Yes. It helped me not to be so worried all the time. Now that he's gone, I keep saying those words to myself, but, well, it isn't the same. I miss your dad."

Like a dam bursting, Freddie leapt out of the chair and hugged my waist. Although he almost knocked the plate out of my hand, no food fell on the floor. I set it on the desk and knelt down to hug him back. He began to cry as his small arms went around my neck. I whispered to him, smelling the shampoo in his hair. "This day stinks. I know. I know." His sobs slowed down, and then he pulled away.

"Why are they having a party because my dad died?" Freddie asked.

"Strange, isn't it? I guess they want people to talk about your dad and hug each other, like we just did, but that doesn't mean you have to go out there. If you feel better in here, that's fine too. Out of all those people, you are the only one who's lost a dad, you know. Just make sure you check in with your mom."

Freddie nodded. "Thank you, Miss Dot."

I picked up my plate. "If you want to stay here, that's fine."

"Okay." He grabbed his bear and returned to the swivel chair, the high back protecting him like a shield.

When I came out of the hallway, leaving Freddie to his quiet place, I ran into Isabella in the corner, conversing with Arturo Galvez. They quickly stepped away from each other, creating a gap that wasn't there before.

"I'm so sorry for your loss, Isabella."

"Yes. Thank you," she answered me dismissively. No doubt, she had heard this phrase countless times in the last few hours. Her gaze turned back to Arturo, a handsome man who oozed masculinity. He was a direct contrast to awkward Milton. I had the impression that whatever Arturo was selling, Isabella was buying it.

Arturo lifted a finger in the direction of the crowd. "Maybe you should go mingle a little more, Isabella. I don't want to take up all your time." It was more of a command than a suggestion.

"Of course." Isabella returned to the crowd.

Arturo was patting his pockets, no doubt looking for cigarettes. I took this moment to ask him a question. "I heard you visited Milton at the hospital. I didn't know the two of you were friends. I can see you and Isabella definitely are much closer than anyone knew."

Arturo stood up straighter, his broad shoulders expanding. "What business is this of yours?"

"It was just something I observed, and so have the police. Out of curiosity, where were you when Milton was killed?"

"Where was I? I was busy at an appointment."

"With whom, may I ask?"

"Again, this is not your business."

"And you know a lot about business, Mr. Galvez. Your company is one of the most successful in Camden."

"It is."

"Something like that takes a lot of hard work and, as Jimmy has told me, 'finagling.'"

"I think we've said enough."

"One more thing. I could be wrong about this, but it looks like there might be a future for you and Isabella. Isabella, who is connected to the Gibsons through her son with Milton."

"So?"

"The Gibsons are a pretty close-knit family, and I wonder how they will feel about her getting involved with you after losing their son?"

I suddenly felt someone standing behind me and jumped slightly. My piece of cake hit the floor.

"Uh, Dot." Al leaned over to pick up the spilled food. "I'm sorry. I thought you saw me."

"Hi, Al. It was nice of you to come to the memorial."

"Well, Milton is the one who made sure that my bid got on the strip mall job. There's a lot of competition out there for a guy like me." Al nodded to Arturo, and Arturo raised his chin. It wasn't exactly a friendly nod, but more like two men acknowledging each other before a fight. Al placed his hand on my elbow. "Could we go talk somewhere?"

"Sure."

Arturo looked relieved by Al's interruption and quickly left the hallway while Al led me over to an empty couch. I set my plate on a side table.

"The nerve of that guy." He looked toward Arturo. "Milton isn't even in the grave yet, and he's making a move on his wife."

I hesitated to tell Al that had likely started way before Milton's death. Maybe it had merely been a mild flirtation that never amounted to anything, but I couldn't be sure. "Isabella needs support right now."

"Yeah, right." His eyes focused on me. "But that's not what I want to talk about. Have you spoken to Ellie? Do you know what's going on with her?"

"Yes. She told me she wasn't sure if she was ready to run off to Vegas to get married. Honestly, Al. Only people in the movies do that kind of thing, and most of them end up running back there to get a quickie divorce." I hesitated. It felt like I was intruding, but I asked anyway. "Why the rush? I thought you were happy to wait until June."

"I was, but it's because of what happened when you went to Dallas. I've never seen Ellie cry like that. I wanted to take her in my arms and protect her. You know? I guess that's where I got the idea about eloping to Las Vegas. I thought that would make her happy again. Get her out of this funk."

I knew Ellie no longer believed in true love and happiness like she had before we got in that taxi. Al was doing all he could to save it. Preserve it. I drew in a breath. "You need to give her some time. She's a little jaded right now, and who wouldn't be after what we saw? I keep seeing the whole scene when I try to go to sleep at night. I've never been so frightened."

Al ran a finger along the crease of his freshly pressed pants. "Don't you see how that won't work? After what happened, I would think it would teach us all that time is precious. None of us knows how much time we have left in this life."

I reached up and touched my necklace. "Trust me on this. She'll come around."

"Dot." Harry Gibson walked over. "Glad you could make it. Milton always liked you." I rose to shake Harry's hand. His eyebrows crinkled together. "That's interesting. Where did you get that necklace?"

Jimmy appeared and stood next to his father. "I thought we threw that away. What are you doing with that?"

I smiled and put the heart between my fingers to show it to Harry and Jimmy. "I cleaned it up. Isn't it pretty?"

Harry stroked his chin. "It's beautiful."

"I'm surprised you even noticed it, but I guess I do play with it without even thinking about it."

Jimmy shook his head. "I never thought of you as a trash digger, Dot." He looked toward the door. "Excuse me. The press is here, and I want to escort that gentleman out."

Ben Dalton stood in the doorway, holding his hat, scanning the crowd. I hoped he was looking for me.

"I'll come with you." I turned back to Al. "Give it time, Al."

"Easy for you to say," he answered with a sad smile.

Jimmy spoke a little too loudly, causing several guests to turn toward the door. "Mr. Dalton, we did not invite you to this function. Kindly make your way out."

Ben gave Jimmy a confident smile. "I thought memorials were open to the public. Don't you want to let me have an outlet for my grief, like everyone else?" His focus bounced to me as I joined Jimmy by the door. "Hi, Dot. Thanks so much for inviting me." His tone softened. "How are you doing, darling?" He stepped beside me and put a possessive arm around my waist. "I'm only glad I could be here for you. I know how upset you've been."

This put me square in the middle between my boss and my boyfriend—no, my friend. A friend I wanted to get to know better, but still, a friend. What was more important? My job or my budding romance with this roving reporter?

"Ben." I pulled his hand from my waist. "You didn't have to come."

"Of course I did, Snookums. You know how much I care." He could have sold old ladies life insurance with the smile he was giving me.

Jimmy's face turned a shade of red I had only seen in a Santa suit. "Dot, we don't need this guy here. He'll print whatever our guests say, and they won't even know it. You want that?"

"What's going on here?" Harry joined in.

"I'm taking care of it, Father," Jimmy assured him. "This gentleman is from the local paper."

"Kindly take your leave, sir. We're grieving here."

I looped my arm through Ben's. "Come on, Snookums. I'll walk you out to your car." Jimmy curled his upper lip and gave me a rough nod as Ben walked out the door. I turned back for my purse and keys and joined him outside.

"Why did you do that?" Ben asked once we stepped outside into the chilly air. Ben returned his fedora to his head and shivered.

I clasped my arms across my chest. "Because I didn't want to lose my job."

"I thought you hated that job."

"I do, but getting fired would be worse. I have to stick it out for as long as I can." It surprised me that somewhere inside, I'd decided about my first job. I wasn't in a good place, and I didn't like my boss's attitude, but I would make the best of it and then leave. This realization gave me peace.

"I guess that's fair. Did you hear anything in there? Do the police know who killed Milton yet?"

"Not yet. If I had to put money on it, I'd say it was Elwood Kirk. Something's fishy about that guy. He was crawling under Jimmy's desk. I'm not totally sure what he was doing, but now, the electrical permit has turned up missing."

Ben scratched his head under the fedora. "You think he murdered Milton because of an electric permit? Man, I thought journalism was ruthless."

"I don't know for sure. It's something that's sticking out right now. There was also something going on with Milton's wife."

Leaning his head forward, Ben smiled. "Would you care to elaborate?"

I realized I'd said too much. Even though Ben and I were becoming close, I still didn't trust him to keep things to himself. "I shouldn't."

Ben's eyes narrowed. "Come on, Dot. You can't dangle a thing like that out there and then drop it."

"Sure I can. Sometimes, when I observe something, I come up with the wrong impression. I'm sure that's what happened in this case." Arturo had been standing close to Isabella, but even though I had my suspicions, it could mean nothing. She was a grieving widow, and he was comforting her. Or something. Whatever it was, I knew Mary and John wouldn't like me spreading rumors about Isabella.

"If I promise I'll keep it to myself, would that help?"

I debated. He looked so trustworthy with those big blue eyes and that Howdy Doody smile. Could I trust him? Should I?

"You wouldn't print anything in the paper?"

"I'd try not to. Is that a good enough answer? I mean, if it's newsworthy, I can't keep it quiet."

I pulled my jacket closer. "Newsworthy. All I need to hear. Have a good day, Ben." I walked to my car in a move that would have made a great silver screen exit, but Mary pulled her car onto the street in front of the Gibson house.

She got out and waved her hands. "Dot! Glad I caught you. How is Isabella doing? Is she okay?"

"Yes, Dot. Why don't you tell all of us how Isabella is doing?" Ben echoed.

"She's keeping it together. Have you learned anything else on the investigation?"

"Yeah," Mary said. "We had a sketch artist go out to the diner to get a description of the man Milton was arguing with."

Ben stepped in front of me, pulling a pad out of his pocket. "Can we get a copy of that sketch for the *Courier*?"

"We've already sent one over to your paper."

"Does it look like anyone you know?" I asked.

"Not really. To be honest, the sketch artist worked with both waitresses who saw the man, and one guy has blond hair, and the other has black. Witnesses often see two different things. It can have to do with the angle they observed the incident, the position of the sun, and even if they needed to put on glasses. You can't be sure."

"So, which one did you send to the paper?" Ben asked.

"We had the sketch artist make a composite. I'm hoping one of the descriptions we had was accurate. If not, we may have put out a wrong description." Mary looked toward the front door of the Gibson house. "I'll have to apologize for being so late." She grimaced and made her way into the house, switching roles from investigator to part of the bereaved family.

Chapter Thirteen

After a long weekend tiptoeing around Ellie's mood, I was almost glad for Monday to roll around. Ben had called and wanted to go to dinner, but then had to cancel at the last minute for a story. I continued my search for the missing permit. If I didn't find it this morning, then that meant a trip to the city building for another copy. I didn't know what was involved in getting a second copy, but surely it had been done before. Contractors weren't known for their organizational skills. In addition to the permit, I couldn't find the submission form Jimmy and I had been working on for the Golden Hammer selection committee. The last time I'd laid hands on it was sometime around Milton's accident. If Jimmy found out it was missing, too, he'd fire me on the spot. It was only Monday, and I was already fed up with my job.

Jimmy and Elwood were out at the building site. They were still clearing the land and preparing to lay the foundation for the strip center. Jimmy's last words were, "Find that permit, Dot. We'll be at the electric hookups before you know it."

I was still searching when Elwood came in a little bit later.

"What's got you in a tizzy?"

"Have you seen the electrical permit? I thought it was right here, but now I can't find it."

Elwood's lip curled into a smile as he watched me squirm. He seemed to be enjoying my failure to locate the permit. I couldn't decide if he had something against me, or if he looked down on all women. He didn't look like the type to have embraced the new women's movement. To Elwood,

I was the "girl" who got coffee and took care of tedious paperwork—the tedious chores that interfered with real work.

Finally, after an hour of searching every file in the drawer and gaining a paper cut, I gave up and went into the city office building. I could check in on my dad while I was there. He worked as the city clerk, and if anybody could help me get an extra copy of the permit, it was him.

Ten minutes later, I popped into Dad's office.

"Dot? What brings you here today?" He wore one of his classic gray suits with a white shirt and a thin navy-blue tie.

"I've lost an electrical permit for the strip mall project. Do you think you could help me get a copy of another one? Jimmy said if I don't come up with it soon, he'll replace me with someone else from the secretarial school." I had spent two long years at the Hudson Secretarial School and knew Jimmy was right—there were plenty of young women ready to take my place. I'd heard Hudson had a new line of electric typewriters which would make typing speeds go through the roof, so new graduates even had a leg up. I had to stick with this job until I could safely leave without it wrecking my resume.

My father arched an eyebrow. "He said that? I don't think I like the sound of this fella."

Mike Morgan might be the city clerk, but he was also a protective father. I tried to placate him. "I'm fine, Dad."

"If you say so." He exhaled and then rose to a filing cabinet behind him. "Give me a few minutes to find it and make a copy. Why don't you head over to the bakery across the street and pick us up a donut?"

I liked the idea of sharing a donut with my dad. "I'd be glad to, and thank you for this."

"Not a problem. Chocolate iced, please. Oh, and don't tell your mother. She thinks I eat too many sweets."

"On my way." As I descended the stairs, I nearly ran into Harry Gibson. He had been looking straight ahead with a glazed look in his eyes.

"I'm sorry. I must not have been looking where I was going."

Harry looked at me for the first time. "Oh, Dot. I didn't see you there. Are you okay?"

"I'm fine." His cheeks looked ruddy. It was cold outside, but judging from the circles under his eyes, I felt like there was more going on. "Are you feeling okay, Mr. Gibson?"

He looked at the floor. "Fit as a fiddle. Well, as fit as I can be now with all these funeral dramatics going on. Raising someone else's child is never easy, but I damn sure never expected to be burying him. My wife is, well, she's not taking it easily." He drew a hand to his forehead and pushed back a shock of silver hair. "You know, I'm not the best fellow around here. I've done some things I'm not proud of with the excuse of doing business. Sometimes, I think losing Milton is the payback."

I'd never seen Harry Gibson this way before and felt genuinely sorry for him. Maybe he wasn't so bad. I tried to reassure him. "The police are working hard on Milton's murder. I'm sure they'll find out who did it."

"Who knows?" He shrugged. "I was never nice to him, mostly because he screwed up so much. It was like he walked around with a rain cloud over his head. I thought he was weak, and if I pushed him a little more, he'd turn out to be the man I wanted him to be."

"Like Jimmy?"

"Yeah. Jimmy's a go-getter kind of guy, and that's what I wanted for Milton."

"When did you hear about Milton's death?"

"I was watching my westerns on ABC. *Stony Burke, The Dakotas, The Rifleman*. Best night on TV."

"Was anyone with you?"

"My wife was in her room. She spends a lot of time resting." Harry shrugged. "I'll let you get back to work."

Twenty minutes later, after enjoying a donut or two with my father, I picked up a copy of the electric permit. "Love you, Dad."

He looked surprised. "I love you too, Pumpkin." The other clerk in the room smiled.

I left before the clerk could tell me how adorable she thought my pet name was and headed to check on Ellie.

When I dropped a couple of donuts by Ellie's dress shop, she was leaning over the counter. She picked over the baked goods, finally choosing one made of plain cake.

"I only have a minute, but I just met up with Milton's father. He finally seems upset."

"I'll bet. Milton's death is still so fresh, and I don't know if they'll ever figure out what happened to him. It could have been anybody. A random stranger. You never know who you're going to run into on public transportation like that. Besides, he was recovering from a concussion. He could have done something or said something that triggered a monster. The world is a scary place."

I had heard that theory twice at the memorial. Everyone loved to think of a murderer being a random stranger. No one from town could have murdered sweet Milton. I could think of at least three people who might commit a crime like that, but in a small town, it wasn't imaginable.

"So, how are you and Al?"

Ellie took a bite of her donut. "The same. We agree to disagree."

"I think it's more like he's agreeing. Did he tell you why he wanted to move up the wedding?"

"Yes." She waved her other hand in the air. "Get this. He wants to be my big, bad protector. Like he's a caveman. Frankly, I don't get it. Look at me." She set her donut down and put her hands to her sides like a model. "I'm thirty-two and run my own business. I live on my own—well, with you—pay my own bills and am doing fine without a man."

"Come on, now. You were willing to marry him last week."

"I was willing to marry him in June. Not December."

I glanced at my watch. "I'd better go."

I decided to run by the construction site on my way back to the office to tell Jimmy I had the electric permit. As I drove up to the site, Jimmy was pacing back and forth, his arms waving in the air, while Elwood stood with his arms crossed. I had hoped things would get better today, but watching the anger in Jimmy's eyes, it would be nothing of the sort. As I left my vehicle and drew closer, I saw the reason for Jimmy's anger. The excavator was front end down in a giant hole in the ground.

"How long will it take us to pull it out? You should have had a truck out here an hour ago. What do I pay you for?" Jimmy shouted. Other workmen stood on the sidelines behind Elwood.

"It takes time to get a heavy-duty tow, boss."

"And when were you going to explain to me how this happened?"

Elwood took off his white Dallas Cowboys ball cap and ran a hand through his dark hair. "I've talked to all the men, sir, and no one knows how it got in the ditch. All I can figure is kids got to it."

"Where was the key?"

"In the office, sir." It was unusual for Elwood to say *sir*. Most of the time, it was Jimmy or boss.

"So, you're trying to tell me that a group of clever children broke into the office leaving not a trace, found the keys, started the excavator, and then dumped it into a hole? What do you take me for? A fool?"

Color flooded Elwood's cheeks. He shrugged his shoulders. "Then your guess is as good as mine."

"Are you sure no one pulled a Milton and tried to do something ahead of schedule? We're digging up septic tanks today, and that hole looks the right size."

Elwood eyed the hole. "Sure, but where's the old septic tank?"

Jimmy gave a staccato shake of his head, as if he'd heard enough. "Unbelievable." He stepped closer to Elwood and wagged his finger in his face. "You'd better have the excavator out of that hole in two hours. Hear me?"

Elwood responded coolly. "I'll do my best."

"Your best isn't good enough. Get it done." Jimmy turned abruptly and faced me, throwing me out of observer mode.

"What?" he snapped.

"I have the electric permit." I held up the piece of paper I was holding, but the wind took it.

"For Pete's sake, Dot," Jimmy yelled as the paper sailed across the dirt.

"I'll get it." I trudged across the ground to retrieve the permit, which landed on a pile of dirt near the hole. Thank goodness it didn't end up in the hole. I snatched it out of the dirt, but as I did, a small white rock fell to the ground. I picked it up, looking at how smooth it was.

"We don't have all day, Dot."

I shoved the rock in my pocket and then held up the permit. "I have it!" I shouted.

"Go put it in the file before you lose it again."

I wasn't sure I liked the idea that the blame for losing the permit was being assigned to me, but I climbed back through the dirt and rushed to the car. I threw the permit into the seat of my car, and started the motor. Once again, I decided that quitting a job this soon would not look good on my resume.

After carefully filing away the electric permit, I resumed my search for the Golden Hammer submission form. At least Jimmy wasn't blaming me for that. Had that been what Elwood had stuck into his pocket when we caught him behind the desk? I wasn't even sure why I hadn't turned the argumentative foreman into Jimmy.

The phone rang, and when I turned from the gray metal filing cabinet to answer the phone, I banged my knee on an open desk drawer. "Ow. Gibson Construction."

"Really?" It was Mary. "That's how you answer the phone over there? No wonder Jimmy's so crazy."

"Hey. Are you at work?"

"I was, but now I have to get over to Isabella's house. She just called and said she's throwing out Milton's stuff. I guess she isn't the weeping widow type."

"What about John?"

"John is at work." She let out an exasperated breath. "Yeah, well, I'm calling you because if she throws all Milton's stuff out on the lawn, I don't think the Gibsons are going to be thrilled about it."

"So, you want me to call Milton's parents?"

"No, actually, I wanted you to come with me and help settle her down and maybe box up some stuff."

"I don't know. This seems like something Milton's folks should do, or Jimmy. Isabella wasn't too happy to see me the last time."

"The last person I want to work with is that hotheaded boss of yours."

"Yet, I do it daily," I said.

"Can you get away with leaving early?"

I glanced at the clock. It was only two in the afternoon, but I hadn't taken lunch after my run to the courthouse and donut shop. If Jimmy asked, I could tell him I was dealing with his dead brother's wife. That might work. "I can give you an hour. No more. I'm already on thin ice after that permit getting lost."

"I'll take it. I'm on my way."

When we knocked on Isabella's front door, she called out from the other side. "One minute."

She opened the door, dressed in a gray sweatshirt with the logo of St. Mary's University of San Antonio printed on the front. She shook her head in disgust. "I knew you couldn't keep out of this." She directed her comment at Mary and then, instead of inviting us in, turned and walked back into the small one-story home, her thin figure leading the way.

"Of course, I couldn't." Mary waved her hands after her. "You can't throw out your husband's belongings so soon after his murder. And what about your son? Going to throw him out too? Do you know how that's going to look to the police? You look like you're glad to be rid of him. Do you see how that looks?"

"I'm not interested in what other people think." She looked over at me and narrowed her gaze. "Why is she here?"

I stepped forward. "Mary asked me. She thought maybe I could get Milton's things and take them to his family."

"Why you? Where are the honorable Gibson goons?" She threw her hands up in the air. "That's perfect. They're so damn important they send their secretary to clean up after he's murdered. Just perfect."

Mary took hold of Isabella's arm. "What is wrong with you? What brought all this on?"

A cloud came over Isabella's features. "Nothing brought this on."

"Tell me. You were all cozied up in a corner with Arturo Galvez at the funeral reception. Does he have anything to do with this? The way you're acting?"

Isabella glared at Mary. "Why is that any business of yours?" She turned her anger toward me. "I'll bet you couldn't wait to tell people about me and Arturo."

I moved a pile of shirts that appeared to have been thrown on the couch and sat down. "What you do is your business."

"That's not fair. She didn't say anything," Mary said, placing her hands on her hips.

"Yeah? Well then, why did my mother call and tell me I had disgraced our family? Why?"

"You think other people didn't notice you at the funeral? For goodness' sakes, you were the grieving widow, and there you were playing footsies with him. Anything you're getting from your mother, you brought on yourself. And erasing Milton from your life doesn't make you look any better."

"And that's where you're wrong. I'm about to make my life a lot better. I'm done being Mrs. Gibson. Arturo says he loves me, and we're going to get married." Isabella's dreamy declaration proved my suspicions about her.

"Does John know about this?" Mary asked.

"Why would I tell my brother anything? I don't need his judgment, and I definitely don't need yours." She turned and took family photos off the wall.

John was a good man and, as I looked at Isabella, I couldn't believe they came from the same family. John treasured his friendship with Milton and the wartime bond they shared. Isabella was trampling all over Milton and any memories they had left of him. She was still young and beautiful, and a second marriage appeared inevitable. A second marriage right after the murder of the first husband would light a scandal in Camden like no other.

Mary scowled and put her hands on her hips. "Has Arturo actually asked you to marry him?"

Isabella's chin lifted. "Not yet, but he told me he loves me. Isn't that enough?"

"It depends," Mary said, with a look of cynicism in her eyes. "How much does he get in return?"

The dreamy look went out of Isabella's eyes. "You have no idea what true love is like. You and John are like two old people. You plod through your days with jobs and children's noses to wipe. It will never be like that with

Arturo."

Although I had been quiet out of respect for Isabella's grief, I took this turn of conversation to ask, "Where was Arturo on the day Milton was killed?"

Isabella drew the corners of her mouth into a frown. "What are you implying? You think Arturo murdered Milton? He couldn't have. He was with me."

"Well," Mary cleared her throat. "If he's professed his love for you, he had a motive. How long were you together on that day?"

"Uh." She looked at her feet. "I don't know. I wasn't exactly watching the clock."

"Could he have slipped out and come back?" I asked.

"I don't know. But no. He would never commit a murder. Arturo is an up-and-coming member of this community. He runs the most successful service company in town, and there is no way he would do anything to hurt that. He's a driven man when it comes to his business, and he's going to be the richest man in town." She looked at Mary. "While you are busy putting patches on the knees of your children's pants, I'll be dancing at parties at the Camden Country Club." From what I knew of the country club, I doubted they would be very welcoming to Isabella.

"That's true," Mary said. "And I'll do whatever I have to for my kids, including sewing on patches, but my question to you is, was Arturo driven enough to kill someone?"

Chapter Fourteen

Mary and I placed Milton's clothes in the trunk of my car. We stowed various belongings, including some of Milton's military medals and family pictures, in the back seat.

As I closed the trunk, Mary stood off to the side. "If you could take these over to the Gibsons', that would be great. Maybe it will help smooth the waters between our two families."

I doubted old shirts would take away the sting of their daughter-in-law jumping into marriage with another man right after the death of their son, but I gave Mary a hopeful smile. "Sure." I checked my watch. "Oh, man. I'm already fifteen minutes late. If Jimmy got back from the site, I'll be looking for another job by tonight." I reached for my keys in my pocket, and my fingers touched the tiny white piece I had found at the construction site. I pulled it out and held it in the palm of my hand.

"What do you think this is? Could it be a bone?"

"Sure." Mary came closer. "I do. Where did you find it?"

"I didn't get a chance to tell you, but someone ditched the excavator in a hole this morning. I was waiting to show Jimmy we had the electrical permit and saw this."

Mary reached out. "Do you mind?" She took the tiny bone in her hand. "You found this at the construction site?" She turned it with her thumb and forefinger.

"Yes. Probably a dog bone."

She cocked her head to one side as she rolled the bone through her fingers. "No chew marks. It's more than likely a bone from somebody's roast, but with what happened to Milton, it might be worth looking into. Do you mind if I take this with me?"

This was exciting. Had I found something relevant? "What are you thinking?"

"I'm thinking this looks like part of somebody's finger or maybe a toe."

I looked at the bone fragment. It could be the tip of someone's finger, or like Mary said, part of some family's dinner. "You can't figure out something like that from looking at it."

"No, but last week I filed a case that had bone chips, and this looks like them. Exactly why were they digging a hole?"

"They have to get the old septic tanks out from behind the houses before they can lay a foundation. We still aren't sure who dumped the excavator, and Jimmy's angry about it."

Mary's lip curled on one side. "That doesn't make sense. Surely they would know who was driving the excavator."

"You would think, but Jimmy said it was the kind of thing Milton would do. He was always trying to impress him by jumping ahead on jobs but didn't always know how to do them, so he screwed up. Maybe there's another Milton on the crew."

"I doubt it, and it's pretty sad he would bring up his dead brother's name." Mary placed the bone in her uniform pocket. "I think I might go over there and check out the site myself."

"And I am going to return to the office and try not to break the speed limit."

"Don't worry about it. You got friends on the force, or at least a friend who can lose the ticket in the filing room."

I touched my throat in mock shock. "Why, Officer Oliva, I can't believe you're saying what I think you're saying?"

Mary laughed and pushed at my shoulder. "Get out of here."

When I unlocked the office door and put the Out to Lunch sign back in the drawer, relief rushed through me that Jimmy wasn't there. I checked the answering service for messages and settled down for an afternoon of typing and filing. I would try to locate the missing paperwork for the Golden Hammer submission. That would make Jimmy happy. My mind drifted to finding Elwood crawling under Jimmy's desk. I rolled my office chair over to Jimmy's desk and started searching through stacks of paper. Jimmy would tell me they were organized stacks, but the documents would be much more organized in files. But until the strip mall project was completed, he wanted to have everything at his fingertips. I sifted through the piles of paper, but the submission form was nowhere to be found. I tried to recall the last time I'd seen it. The submission required a list of all building projects for the last year. The Golden Hammer committee wanted to see everything. Needless to say, it was a giant piece of research that had taken much of my time since coming to work for Gibson Construction. I couldn't believe it would have disappeared so easily. After ten minutes of searching, I grew frustrated. I would have to come back to it later.

I made a call to Milton's house, and Isabella answered on the first ring. "Hello?" Her voice was low and sultry. Had she been expecting a call from Arturo?

"Hi. It's Dot. I was wondering if I could ask you a question about Milton?"

Her tone immediately changed. "I suppose."

"Did he ever bring home paperwork?"

"Yes. Why do you care?"

"Oh, uh. We're missing something here, and I was wondering if maybe he took it home. It's the submission for the Golden Hammer award. Did he ever talk about that?"

"How would I know? He rambled on about work all the time. That didn't mean I was listening."

"Okay. Well, if you see it lying around anywhere, we'd appreciate you bringing it to Gibson Construction. Thanks for your help." I hung up and thought about the rotten luck of it going missing. Although it was typical for the kinds of things that happened when Milton was alive. I did have a carbon copy of the submission form, but re-typing it would take time. If I were smart, I'd start now.

Jimmy came blustering through the door. "Oh, no. Now you're sitting at my desk? Trust me, there will never be a successful construction company with a woman at the helm. None of you broads could handle it."

Ignoring his rudeness, but feeling anger nonetheless, I quickly stood up and pushed my chair back to my desk. "I was looking for our Golden Hammer submission. I haven't been able to find it anywhere."

Jimmy hung his coat on a hook. "Are you kidding? You've lost that too?"

"Not quite sure if I'd call it lost yet."

"My god, Dot. This sounds like something my brother would have done."

"You're right. I hate to say it, but this is the kind of thing that happened when Milton was alive. We can't exactly blame him for it now."

"Nope. I guess the blame's on you this time." He walked over to the percolator and tilted it to pour a cup of coffee. When nothing came out, he scowled. "Why isn't there any coffee?"

"Oh, I'm sorry. It was just me, and I didn't make any. I can make another pot." I hurried to the sideboard where the percolator and coffee supplies sat.

"I should think so."

"This is going to sound crazy." I stalled for a moment. What I was about to tell him would put Elwood in hot water, and Elwood scared me.

"Out with it," Jimmy said, rolling his hand in the air.

I bit my bottom lip, took a breath, and blurted out, "I have absolutely no idea why he would be doing this, but do you think Elwood could have taken the submission form?"

Jimmy gave me a look that would have made me shrivel up on the first day. Now, I buffered it off. "Why would he do that? Elwood is a loyal Gibson employee. Don't try to blame your disorganization on him."

"Where was he working before he came here?"

"Sawyer Home Builders, and we were damn lucky to get him. He was over there for years. I think he might even be related to someone in the company, but I'm not sure who."

"Why did he leave?"

"Who the hell cares? Without him, I never could have fixed all the messes Milton made around here."

"True, but just out of curiosity, when did all that start? Was Milton always causing problems?"

"I don't know. What is wrong with you? You seem to be working awfully

84

hard to get yourself out of a jam."

"Will Sawyer Home Builders be in the running for the Golden Hammer?"

"Of course, they will." Jimmy put a hand to his chin, and his expression suddenly changed. "Son of a bitch." Jimmy slammed his hand on the desk. "You think Elwood is trying to get Sawyer to win?"

"That's why we found him under your desk. At least it's a theory. If he is related to someone over there, maybe blood is thicker than water."

"I'll fire that rat bastard. No one cheats on Jimmy Gibson."

I was glancing at the clock when Elwood came in. It was five minutes until five, and Jimmy had been stewing behind his desk for the last half hour. I thought about getting my purse and making my way to the door, but when I pulled it out of my desk drawer, Jimmy raised his hand.

"Don't go yet, Dot," Jimmy commanded. "I want you to be here for this."

I wanted to be anywhere but here at the moment, but I sat back down in the chair and waited.

"What's up, boss?" Elwood strode toward Jimmy's desk, his mood jovial. "Did you see how far we got today? Once we got the excavator out of the hole, we got all the septic tanks out. I don't think we've lost much time at all."

Elwood was good at telling Jimmy what he thought he wanted to hear. He delivered his news with a confident smile—a smile with a slight tremor in it, but looking from the outside, he seemed like a man in control.

Jimmy nodded as he took in the progress report. "Good to hear. Did anyone ever confess to dumping the excavator in that hole?"

"Nope. I asked the men, and they all swore they didn't do it. Frankly, I believe every one of them. I don't know how it happened, but it wasn't our guys."

"How long have you worked for us, Elwood?"

Elwood stepped closer. "Almost a year. I love it here."

"And you were at Sawyer before this, right? Tell me again why you left there?"

Elwood straightened. "You know how it is. Always someone who has no idea what they're doing. I couldn't take it anymore. It wasn't like here."

"Yeah, but we made all kinds of mistakes over here."

"That was Milton."

"Was it? Tell me, aren't you related to someone in that company?"

Elwood shifted to one foot. "Not important. My loyalty's here."

"Who are you related to, Elwood?"

Elwood looked down, then at me, and then at Jimmy. "My father-in-law is John Sawyer." The air in the office seemed to thicken after his answer. "Listen." He crossed his arms as a snarl came across his features. He might have been caught, but I could tell it did not cow him. "I get the work done. This hasn't been a problem until you hired this girl. Since she's been here, there's been nothing but trouble. First Milton gets murdered, and now this. I'm not the problem." He turned and pointed at me. "She is."

Jimmy closed his eyes and then rubbed at his forehead. "You're right. You're a good worker, and you've managed our men well. It's just this submission for the Golden Hammer coming up missing is curious."

"Has it? Honest, boss, as far as Sawyer goes, no one should have to work for their own father-in-law. You, of all people, know how hard it is to work with family."

"Tell me about it," Jimmy agreed.

"I knew you'd get it."

Jimmy turned to me. "Pack up, sweetie. We don't need your nosy kind around here."

What? He was firing me? "Mr. Gibson. Jimmy. You can't be serious."

"No," Jimmy said. "I don't know. A lot of things have happened here since you signed on. Terrible things."

"Exactly." Elwood crossed his arms and grinned.

"Go home." Jimmy gestured toward the door. "Settle down. It's not like that. I want everyone to go home so I can think about this. I don't want to fire you, Elwood. You are a damn fine foreman. But you have to admit you should have told me Sawyer was your father-in-law."

"You're right."

"Damn straight, I am." He shook his head, his eyes downward. "Go home. Both of you."

When I walked into my apartment, I was still flabbergasted at the way things had turned out. I could get fired, and it wouldn't be fair. I found Ellie bent over the coffee table, a stack of colorful brochures in front of her.

"What would you think of me going into the Peace Corps? You know, take a year off and help people." She raised one hand in the air as she quoted the words of John F. Kennedy. "Ask not what your country can do for you, but what you can do for your country."

"You want to go into the Peace Corps?"

"I'm thinking about it."

"What about Al?"

"What about him?"

"I thought you two were getting married."

Ellie shook her head and put down the brochure. She brushed at the air as if pushing an invisible Al to a corner in the room. "He'll be here. Right now, I'm young and full of energy. This could be a year that will change my life."

Whatever was going on with Ellie had deepened. I felt the hopelessness that lingered after the death of the president, but with Ellie, good old optimistic Ellie, it was twisting some of the good out of her. "I hate to be rude, but I'm worried about paying the rent here without you."

"I know that's a problem. I'll try to help you out some on that, but I'll probably be having some expenses of my own," Ellie answered.

"Have you talked to your parents about this?"

Ellie's mother was a maverick in the community. Aunt Mavis worked as a nurse at the hospital, and they had reprimanded her more than once for helping people outside of work hours. "Old people go home, and sometimes they don't have family there to take care of them." Ellie's mom would spend weeks going over after a long shift to make sure the person got dinner and was recovering. Maybe this idea about the Peace Corps stemmed from that.

Ellie gave a little laugh. "No, but I'm sure my mother would approve."

"What about your dad?"

"Dad might be a little tougher, but he never stopped my mother from helping people."

"She never gave your dad the chance. Your mother can be pretty obstinate."

Ellie chuckled. "And you wonder where I get it."

I walked over and put my hands on Ellie's. "Promise me you'll think about this before you start packing."

"What's to think about? No matter what evil force is out there, I can fight it. I can make a change in the world and carry on what Jack Kennedy started." Her eyes were focused, her jaw firm. She meant it. The death of the president might have been an international incident, but something had also changed in little Camden, Texas. I now doubted the lyrics sung by Frank Sinatra that I loved so much. A little ole ant can't really move a rubber tree plant.

Chapter Fifteen

The phone rang with an irritating clacking sound. "Let it ring. It's Al. He's been calling me all day." Ellie, who used to jump off the couch when Al called, stayed still.

"Why don't you answer it?"

Ellie pushed back on the couch, tipping her chin upward. "And have the same argument over again? Isn't that the definition of insanity? Al thinks if he talks to me enough, he can get me to change my mind."

The phone continued, and I felt a headache coming on. After the day I had today, putting up with that phone would make me either suicidal or homicidal. I picked up the receiver.

"Is this Al?"

"Hi, Dot. Let me speak to Ellie, would you?"

"She says she doesn't want to talk to you."

"I don't know what to do," he said after a pause. "I thought everything was fine."

I'll admit it. Even though I loved my cousin, I felt sorry for Al. Ellie and Al were one couple who, for the last ten years, went to everything together. Picnics, holiday gatherings, church services. They were always together. Seeing one without the other made people in Camden ask if one of them was ill. "I'm sorry."

"I just don't understand," he murmured. "Maybe you could talk to her?"

"I've tried."

"Well, maybe if I could tell you how I feel, you could relate it to her. She won't listen to me."

"I guess I could try." I glanced at Ellie, who was listening to every word on my side of the phone call.

"Thank you, Dot. I can't seem to get through to her, and she listens to you. Or at least she used to. Can you meet me for coffee?"

I hadn't eaten supper, and more coffee would give me the shakes. "If you buy me a burger, too."

When I hung up, Ellie was standing behind me. I hadn't even heard her rise from the couch, but it showed that even though she said she didn't care, she did. "What did he say?"

"I thought you weren't talking to him, so what does it matter?"

Ellie's mouth thinned. "You're right. Whatever Al does is Al's business. He's a free man."

"Great. I'm going out to dinner."

"With Al?"

"You don't care, remember?"

When we met at the local McDonald's, I went over to Al's car and sat in the passenger seat. A young woman I recognized from secretarial school came over on roller skates.

"Hey, Dot." She rolled over and stopped herself by grabbing the driver's side window opening. "It's good to see you."

"You too. How's school?"

"Now that Miss Robinson is gone, it's a lot better. I guess we have you to thank for that. I still can't get my typing score up, though. I sure hope I'm not doomed to work at this place for the rest of my life."

I remembered this girl. She'd had trouble in all her classes, which might also explain why she was making a living as a carhop. We gave her our orders, and then Al pled his case.

"Has she mentioned anything about this before?" Al asked. "I mean the Peace Corps? That's for college kids. Not a mature woman like Ellie."

"No, this is the first I've heard of it, but it doesn't seem totally foreign. She's taking after her mother, wanting to help others."

"It's her mother. Nothing against her, and well, she helped old lady McCoy. We worked on her electric, and that woman could screech the feathers off an owl, but that didn't faze Ellie's mom. The thing is, she helps out folks right here in town. She doesn't have to go to another country to be a caregiver."

A blue Corvette with a white stripe down the hood pulled up in the empty park next to us. I knew whose car that was and hoped he wouldn't look over. Elwood Kirk rolled down his window to place his order. When he did, his eyes flashed in my direction. I had my window rolled up, but Elwood motioned with his finger, demanding I roll it down.

"Funny meeting you here. I was just thinking about you. Well, maybe not so much as I was just cursing you for all the trouble you've caused me." He glanced over at Al. "And now I see you're stepping out with one of our contractors. Hmmm. I wonder what Jimmy would think of that."

Al leaned over. "It's not like that. I'm her cousin's fiancé."

Elwood's mouth curved into a leer. "My, my, Dot. You are a woman of many secrets. With that blond hair and those big eyes, I took you for the dumb Marilyn Monroe type." He held up both hands in front of him. "My mistake, but I'll tell you one thing I'm not mistaken about. Your nosiness is about to get me fired from a sweet job."

"That's quite enough," Al said.

Elwood sneered. "What're you going to do about it?" Elwood opened his car door and advanced on Al's car.

I reached out to Al. "Don't. Let me handle this." I opened my car door and faced Elwood. He towered over me, but I tried to stand straighter. It was a Mighty Mouse moment. "You try anything, don't forget, I have a very good friend on the police force who will make sure you don't get away with it."

He crossed his arms and then looked at me suspiciously. He knew some of the boy's club on the police force. "And who would that be?"

"Mary Oliva." Elwood didn't look impressed, so I rephrased it to make it sound better. "Officer Mary Oliva."

He shook his head. "Who the hell is that?"

"Never you mind, but I'll make sure that she's aware of your threats. Also, I have Al here to back me up. An eyewitness."

Elwood laughed. "Sure." He mimicked my voice and shook his head from side to side like a bobblehead. "An eyewitness. You bet, Joe Friday. There's something you're forgetting. Jimmy ain't too pleased with you either. We may both be out of a job. I'll find more work, but for you it's going to look pretty bad. A fresh secretary school candidate out on her ass before she even works two months."

My friend returned with the hamburgers and placed the tray on Al's window. She glanced at Elwood. "Sir, if you'll return to your car, I'll take your order."

Elwood stood for a second more, giving me a hard stare. "No thanks. I don't much care for the clientele here."

He got back behind the wheel and screeched out of the parking lot.

"You sure made him angry. What's his beef?" the waitress asked.

"He's about to lose his job." I got back in Al's car.

"If I only had one," she lamented, then rolled away.

"Seems like nobody's happy with the way their life is going anymore," Al said.

I unwrapped my hamburger and took a bite. "Yep."

Chapter Sixteen

The next morning, I came into the office early, hoping to make a good impression on Jimmy. If my job hung in the balance, I could at least be on time. If I found myself fired, what would I do next? My dad told me they were always looking for secretaries at the city building, and he knew quite a few lawyers. That was comforting, but there was no guarantee any of them would want me. Even if I went that route, what would I say about my first job? My old typing teacher, Miss Robinson, who never liked me anyway, would have predicted something like this would happen. My typing and filing abilities were at the top of my class, but my problem was I was more than that. The tedium of office work did not stimulate my mind. As I toiled through the day-to-day grind of my first job, I discovered that maybe the thing I trained for wasn't enough for me. If I kept thinking like this, I'd be signing up for the Peace Corps with Ellie.

Jimmy and Elwood showed up together, laughing at something they were discussing outside. My heart leapt. Was it over? Had Elwood gotten to Jimmy and convinced him that all their troubles concerned me?

"Good morning, Jimmy." I tried to put on that nothing-to-see-here voice. Jimmy turned toward me, looking like a child had disturbed him.

"Morning."

Elwood chose not to respond, but he gave me a surly look. No doubt he'd been busy selling Jimmy on his value.

Jimmy walked over and poured coffee into a small thermos he had been carrying. "We'll be out at the site most of the day. I'll look at my messages later."

"Yes, sir." The phone rang, and I answered it on the first ring. "Gibson Construction."

Jimmy and Elwood returned to their conversation, reveling in some past project they stole from another contractor. I strained to hear the caller over their voices.

"Hey Dot, it's Mary. I just wanted you to know that the bone you found at the construction site is human. It's part of a little finger. You need to tell your boss the police are coming out to the site today to look for any other fragments."

I nestled the phone against my shoulder and looked over at Jimmy, who was in the middle of a humorous story. "Mr. Gibson?" He continued talking, so I repeated his name. "Mr. Gibson?"

"What?" he answered sharply.

"The police are on the phone. They're heading to the job site."

"Whatever for?"

"They, well, I found a little bone out there the other day. I gave it to Officer Oliva, and she said it's human. They want to search the ground for any other bone fragments."

"Holy hell. Are you kidding me?" He stormed over, Elwood following closely. "What the hell were you doing digging through my dirt and then running off to the cops with it?"

I stuttered. "It was just something I picked up. I didn't know it was human."

"That's it, Dot. I've been more than patient. In construction, some people make your projects go faster, and some make them go slower. I can't stay in business with you working for me. Now we're losing another day on this project. You're fired, Dot. The answering service will get the phone. Pack up your stuff and get out of here."

Jimmy stormed out, slamming the door. I returned to the police on the line and let them know my boss had been informed, then hung up. It had happened. He had fired me from my first job. What would I tell my parents? I stood there in shock, and then went in the back to dig up a box to pack my things. I felt like a failure. A total screw-up. I was sad and angry, but as I dug for a box, underneath the sadness, like a crocus waiting for spring, a new feeling was emerging. I couldn't have ever imagined continuing to work for Jimmy Gibson. Especially now that he was buddy-buddy with Elwood, a man who admitted lying to him. Hiding the connection to Sawyer Home Builders would have been unforgivable if it were anyone else. Why did Jimmy forgive Elwood, but I stayed in trouble? Maybe it was a bond between men in construction. Jimmy worked around men and preferred the company of men.

I found a box and put my few belongings inside. I grabbed my coat from the coat rack, noticing that Jimmy had left his coffee thermos on the counter in his fit of anger. In some ways, he was just like his brother. I picked it up and threw it into the box. I'd run it out to the construction site, although I had no idea why I was doing a favor for the man who had just fired me. I still had Milton's thermos at home. It needed to be rinsed, but I would put it in the trunk with the clothes I had been planning to deliver today. After that, I would close the book on my association with the crazy Gibson family.

When I pulled up to the demolition site, the police were there, pulling out rakes to run across the dirt in search of evidence. Maybe coming out here was not such a good idea. Mary, who was not just standing guard this time, stepped over to me.

"They let you be a part of this?" I asked.

"I demanded it, seeing as I'm the one who showed them the bone fragment. I was surprised myself. Maybe things are changing for the better over there for women, or maybe for Mexicans. Either way, here I am." She looked down at the red plaid thermos in my hand. "Ah, such a good little secretary, you bring your boss coffee."

"He just fired me."

"What?"

"Yeah. He wasn't too happy that I turned that bone over to you, and now the police search is going to slow down the project."

Mary's eyes widened. "Then why are you doing that jerk a favor?"

"I really don't know." I was as amazed as Mary sounded. "Let me get this over with."

Jimmy was standing with an officer in a deep discussion when I walked up. "Here, Jimmy. You forgot your coffee." As I handed him the thermos, the chain of my necklace gave way, and the small heart hit the dirt.

Jimmy leaned over to pick it up. "Looks like that old thing is past its time after all."

"Thanks." I held out my hand.

"Listen. I was pretty rough on you back there." Had he changed his mind about firing me the same way he changed his mind about Elwood?

"Let me take this to a jeweler for you to get it fixed." He put the necklace in his pocket. "It's the least I could do. Now that you're without a job, you can't afford it, anyway." His words sounded kind and comforting, but something about it didn't ring true. Why was he doing this? Did Jimmy Gibson have a guilty conscience under all that bluster?

"You don't need to do that." I kept my hand out, hoping to get the necklace back.

Jimmy patted his pocket. "Sure I do."

An officer I didn't recognize approached us. "You are the young lady who found the bone? Right? Friend of Mary's?"

"Yes."

"Can you tell me exactly where you were standing when you found it?"

"Sure." I walked over to the location where the first house stood. "It was right about here. The excavator had fallen into a hole, and I found it when I was chasing a piece of paper."

He followed her and looked around. "An excavator fell into a hole. How did that happen?"

"Nobody seems to know," Jimmy said from behind us. "I guess we have two cases you need to solve for us, but I know the Camden police will be on it."

Elwood was leaning against a pickup truck with a few of the other workers. I saw him point in our direction, and then the men laughed. He had to be telling them Jimmy had fired me. This was awful, and I needed to get away from this whole situation. I didn't deserve to be fired, and I sure didn't have to put up with Elwood. "If that's all you need, I need to go start looking for another job, seeing as Mr. Gibson here just fired me."

"Is that so?" the policeman asked. "And you still brought him his thermos." He scratched at his chin. "Charitable."

"Isn't it, though?" I gave a little grin and headed for my car, hoping no one noticed the slight tremble in my voice. Once in the car, I felt the tears coming but tried to start the car without wiping my eyes. It was time to pound the pavement, but this time I'd be interviewing my future employer as much as they were interviewing me. I'd had it up to here with hotheaded bosses and crooked foremen.

Chapter Seventeen

The worst had happened. The root of this feeling of failure sank deep into my soul. I had tried to believe in myself, my abilities, my future, even when others didn't. Today I had lost even my own internal voice. I needed my mother. Just like scraping my knee as a kid, I needed a maternal Band-aid. I made my way to the library.

"I never liked that man," my mother said as she shelved a book. "He's never checked a book out here. Did you know that? He reads the paper because it's free. Who knows what he's been reading, or if he's reading at all?"

"So, this is how you evaluate people?" I laughed. "By their book checkouts?"

"You can tell a lot about a person by what they're reading. I know who likes mysteries, who reads romances, and who has a nasty little medical problem they're not telling other people about. It's all there in black and white."

I shuddered to think someone could know all about you, just by knowing what materials you were searching out and reading. Thank goodness librarians generally kept that information to themselves. It wouldn't be good if somebody got to the drugstore and was suddenly redirected to hemorrhoid creams. What would the world be like if anyone could find out your business? Business. Just the word reminded me of the predicament I was in, now unemployed. "What am I going to do now? I've just started paying my own rent, and if Ellie goes off to join the Peace Corps, I'll have to find another roommate."

My mother shelved the last book from the tan metal rolling cart and made a quick pivot toward me. "You'll find another job." She said it as though finding a new job were as easy as picking up an ice cream sundae at a soda fountain.

"But I got fired from my first job."

"Did you ever question Jimmy about the last secretary he hired?"

"No." I hadn't been told anything about the person I replaced. I had been so happy to get the job, I didn't question why there was an opening. Now that I thought about it, it was strange that no one had been there to train me. Jimmy plunked me down behind the desk and expected me to know everything on my first day. That was when I made friends with Milton. He was the only one who took time to show me where things were.

"See. I'll bet with his attitude he goes through a secretarial school graduate every month. No one wants to work for a man with a temper." I followed her as she pushed the cart back to the checkout desk. "You got off lucky getting out of that place, especially with everything going on over there."

She returned to her place behind the desk. I leaned my elbows on the counter, a stance I had taken since I was tall enough to do it. "You're saying don't worry."

"Don't worry about what?" Ben loped forward from the stacks holding a book, his familiar coat hanging open and his shirttail sticking out on one side. I felt myself blushing. Why did I have this reaction whenever I saw the man? He was a little too tall, gangly, and his mahogany brown hair had a way of curling over his forehead that was adorable.

"Jimmy fired me."

His head bobbed forward slightly. "He fired you? For what?"

I explained about the bone I found at the construction site.

"You found a bone, and you didn't bother to call me? I thought we were friends."

"It happened so quickly."

Ben put his book on the counter and spoke quickly to my mother. "I need to check out. I have a story to write."

Mother picked up the book and read the cover. *The Shoes of the Fisherman* by Morris West. "You're lucky to get this one. It's been on the bestseller list. It asks some deep questions." She shot a look at me and nodded with a smile. "It's good you're keeping up on what people are reading today. You must be

99

a very smart cookie. It's so interesting what people read."

Ben stared down at the floor for a minute and then glanced up, looking a little embarrassed. "I try."

After she finished stamping the book, Ben picked it up and turned to me. "Can I convince you to drive back to the construction site with me so you can tell me about the bone fragment?"

I scratched her head. "I don't know. Jimmy isn't going to want to see me again, especially if we're going to be talking about what I did to slow down this job."

He paused and then went on. "Okay, that's fair. Can you meet me at the lunch counter at noon? I'll buy you lunch."

My mother's smile blinded me. An observer through fiction, she was now observing real life.

"I guess so. I have nothing better to do. I was planning on reading the paper here to get job leads from the classifieds, so I'll meet you then."

"Very good," Ben said.

"Very good," Mother echoed. She stamped the book in a staccato fashion and gave me a knowing look.

At noon, I sat at the lunch counter and stirred my Coke with a straw as I waited for Ben. The classifieds had yielded help wanted ads for a payroll clerk at an oil company, and a position selling radio ads on commission. Living in a small town had its advantages, but a limited job market made it hard to find work.

"Sorry, I'm late." Ben took the red vinyl stool next to me and set his fedora on the counter. "I was trying to get a statement from your old boss, and he kept putting me off."

"Did he ever talk to you?"

"Yeah, sure he did. I'm glad I already know how to spell 'No comment.'"

"Sounds like him." I took a drink of my Coke.

"I'm not worried. I have a former disgruntled employee who wants to spill the beans. They're the best kinds of interviews." He flashed me a smile that made my heart melt a little.

Even with all his journalistic charm, I couldn't help rolling my eyes. "No comment."

"Are you serious? Why would you say that? This is a fantastic opportunity to get back at your boss. Put the screws to him. Let him know he can't shut you up because he fired you." Ben gave a jerky, repeated nod, reminding me of those little dog statues people put in the back windows of their cars.

"I'm not putting the screws to anyone. What good would that do? He has enough problems without me trying to make it worse. As much as I hate to admit it, he had grounds to fire me. I slowed his work down. I'm supposed to be there to speed it up, but first there was the missing Golden Hammer submission form and the electrical permit, and then I went and discovered a part of a skeleton on his behind-schedule project. I'm an albatross around his neck."

"Fine. I appreciate your honest self-appraisal, Dot. Still, can you tell me about finding the bone fragment. How big was it?"

"It was little, like the size of a small marble. I wasn't even sure it was a bone at first."

"Whatever made you pick it up?"

The lunch counter waitress appeared. "What can I get you folks today?"

"I'll have the grilled cheese," I said.

"Uh, give me a tuna sandwich, and don't overdo the lettuce," Ben added.

The waitress recorded our orders in a small notepad and then ripped off the page, attaching it to a round turnstile behind the counter.

"Ben Dalton. What would your mother say? You need your vegetables." I gently nudged him with my elbow.

"My mother isn't here, so I guess she'll stay quiet for the moment. Now, go on with your discovery of the bone."

"Not much to tell. It was behind the first house they had demolished. First, you have to know that someone dumped the excavator in a hole and then ran off."

Ben looked confused. "What?"

"No one knows who dumped the excavator, and Jimmy was on the warpath when it happened. We think one of the men may have been trying to score some points by doing extra work, then got the excavator stuck but didn't want to tell anyone. Could have been someone who knew Elwood's job was in danger, and there was a chance for advancement."

"Why would Elwood's job be in danger?"

I looked around. "This part is off the record for the paper. Understand? Elwood's father-in-law runs Sawyer Home Builders. Competition for the Golden Hammer. And he didn't disclose that to Jimmy when he came to work for him."

Ben threw his hands in the air. "The notorious Sawyer gang. Will it ever end?"

I laughed at the serious face he was making. "Stop. Both of our jobs were on the line, but Jimmy conveniently forgot about Elwood hiding the fact he could be a spy for Sawyer, and the next day, they were slapping each other on the back and laughing as if nothing had ever happened."

"That's weird."

"I think it was a man-to-man thing. You know. Brothers in construction?"

"Actually, I don't know. The only reason someone might change their mind about something is because the other person has something on them, and they can't risk being exposed. Hypothetically."

That thought made sense. "What would Elwood have on Jimmy?"

"Jimmy doesn't seem to like to slow down for anything. Maybe he's cut corners on the buildings they've done together," Ben pointed out.

"I hadn't thought of that, but if so, that leads us to more questions. Like, who does the bone belong to, and who killed Milton?"

There was a flicker in Ben's eyes. "Do you think they're connected?"

"I don't know. I thought this all pointed to Arturo Galvez, with Isabella dumping Milton's belongings and declaring her love for Arturo."

"So how does finding the bone figure in?"

"I found it when a piece of paper got away from me. Jimmy started yelling, so I put it in my pocket. The thing was, it was too smooth to be a pebble, you know?"

The waitress arrived with the lunch plates, slipping the bill under Ben's plate. When she stepped away, Ben said, "Arturo Galvez. I can see that I need to spend more time with you. You're a fount of information for this reporter."

Although I was pleased he wanted to be around me more, I wasn't so sure I wanted my movements documented in the local paper.

"Don't print this, but Isabella is moving on."

"That was fast."

"Too fast. John and Mary are livid."

"You'd think her being John's sister, they'd be on her side."

I thought about the times I'd seen John and Milton together, arm in arm, talking about their time in Vietnam. John had more fondness for Milton's friendship than Isabella did for their love. "John and Mary loved Milton. Isabella is different. She's more ambitious. I don't think she knows herself what would make her happy."

"Arturo is the one with the plumber, electrician, whatever business, right? He's a considerable success in this town, that's for sure. Maybe that's what she finds so appealing about him. Milton wasn't any of those things."

"No, he wasn't, but he was a good man and was becoming a dear friend."

Ben nodded. "Yes, he was, but someone wanted him dead."

Chapter Eighteen

After lunch, I still had Milton's clothes in my trunk and decided to drop them off at the Gibson house. I was breaking ties with this family, and the sooner I completed this last task, the better. I remembered I'd left Milton's thermos at my apartment, so I stopped there first to get it. Isabella obviously didn't want Milton's things, but his mother might want it. When I picked up the thermos, I heard the swishing of the coffee Milton had been drinking before the accident. I felt a twinge of sadness, remembering Milton filling up his thermos for a normal workday. He had no idea he'd be dead within the week.

I went to the kitchen and poured the contents in the sink. There were yellow clumps in the coffee. Milton drank his coffee black, so the clumps couldn't be creamer. Could it be mold? I'd never seen mold that color. This looked suspicious. Milton seemed normal before he got hit by the beam, and then he wasn't. I grabbed a spoon out of the drawer and scooped up some of the residue from the sink. Mary had come through on the bone fragment. She might do the same with this. Had Milton seen these yellow clumps floating around in his coffee? If his coffee had been poisoned, but he only took a small sip, that might explain why he was loopy, but not asleep. Whatever it was, Mary might know someone who could look at this. How could I save this potential piece of evidence? If only someone would invent little bags made of the same material as waterproof rain bonnets. That would be perfect. I had nothing like that, so tried to contain the yellow globs in a handkerchief. It would have to do.

When Harry Gibson opened his front door, I greeted him with a stack of

Milton's clothes folded over my arms. "Hey, Isabella was cleaning out her house, and well...." I couldn't tell the father of a dead son that his wife was dumping his belongings out in the trash. "...she wanted you to have these things."

"I'll just bet she did." From the expression on Harry's face, I could tell he wasn't buying it.

"Can I come in?"

He stretched his arm out in welcome. "Sure. Bring them in. Put them on the couch until I can figure out what to do with them. Jimmy could wear some of these shirts. They're about the same size. Milton was always a little taller, though."

I laid the pile of clothing over a deep orange couch and went out to my car for the rest of Milton's belongings.

Harry followed me, and I handed him a pair of Milton's work boots and a winter coat.

"This was truly kind of you to do this. Can I get you a cold drink, a cup of coffee?"

I was about to say no, but something told me he could use the company. It might not be a good idea to leave him alone with the clothing of a son he would never see again. Harry could be gruff, but I had to consider he had just lost a child. "Sure."

"I'll be just a minute," he said with a smile. "Come on in."

I stood quietly and could hear cabinets opening in the kitchen. Here in the living room, family pictures populated the mantle. There was one with Harry's wife sitting in front of Jimmy, Harry, and Milton. Next to it was a picture of just his wife and another woman who looked to be a little older than Mrs. Gibson. I picked up the frame and examined the woman in the photograph closely.

"Memories on a shelf." Harry was back with cups of coffee. "That's all I have left of Milton now. If you look at me in that family picture, I thought I had it all. I had a new construction company, a beautiful wife, and two handsome sons."

As Harry talked, I realized there was much more to this man than the drive

I saw in Jimmy. He had a soft side, a trait I was sure his son didn't inherit.

"Everything seems so easy when your kids are little. Sometimes Milton seemed like a stranger to me, he was so different from Jimmy. He was more like his mother. Sensitive. You know the type. Then, Milton married a woman who was clearly a gold digger. She wanted the benefits of the Gibson success. I don't think she ever cared for my son. At least we got little Freddie out of it."

"What about Jimmy? Has he ever been married?"

Harry handed me a cup. "Twice. Both times they didn't make it a year. My oldest son is a bit of a bully."

I nodded and tried to give Harry a look of surprise. Calling him a "bit of a bully" was an understatement.

Harry took a sip of his coffee and gazed at the photograph. "He was like that from the day he was born, especially when I married Milton's mother." He blew out a sigh. "So many regrets. They don't tell you getting older means you can't go back and fix things anymore."

I refocused on another photo as I placed the family picture on the fireplace mantel. "Who is that with your wife?"

His lips thinned. "That was Celeste. Those two would start talking about books, and I got about as much attention as a stick of furniture. I never could see what all the fuss was about."

"It's good to have a friend like that." I thought of my cousin Ellie. We had always been close, just not lately. Not since we'd witnessed the assassination. It suddenly dawned on me that I hadn't told Mr. Gibson that Jimmy fired me. "I guess I should tell you Jimmy fired me today. That's partly why I wanted to bring Milton's things to you."

Harry drew his bushy eyebrows together. "Why did he fire you?"

"I found a bone at the construction site, and now the police are out looking for more, so of course, work has been halted until they finish. Jimmy said I keep delaying the job."

"Are you kidding me? A bone? Jimmy hasn't called me about it. That boy." He stood. "I'm sorry. I'm going to have to cut this short."

"It's okay."

"Thanks for bringing the clothes by, especially when you certainly don't owe anything to this family anymore. You can find your way out."

After being so rudely dismissed by Harry, I decided I would take the remnants of the yellow substance from Milton's thermos over to Mary. When I walked into the Camden Police Department, Mary sat behind the desk with a stack of folders.

My friend looked up and smiled. "What brings you in here this time of day?"

"I'm going to have a lot more time on my hands from now on, but I'll get to that later. I brought you something. When I emptied out Milton's thermos, I found these clumps floating around in it." I unfolded the handkerchief, expecting to show her the little yellow dots. Instead, they had melted into the cloth.

"I can barely see anything."

The substance had been absorbed by the cloth. "There really was something there. You see, Milton drinks his coffee black, so there should have been no reason for anything powdery to be in his drink."

"And why would this be important to me?"

"Because this is the coffee that he was carrying around the day he walked out in the middle of the demolition. Remember, he seemed fine when he talked to me earlier, but later he looked like he was in some sort of daze."

"So, what are you saying?"

"Could it be that someone tried to drug Milton?"

"Why?"

"I'm not totally sure of that, but if someone did dump a drug into his coffee, he would undoubtedly taste it. He never added cream or sugar, so it would ruin the taste of the coffee. Maybe they were trying to kill him, but because the coffee tasted bad, he only drank a small amount."

Mary's coworker, Officer Jerry, came over. I had only been to the police department a few times before, but Jerry recognized me. "Back again?"

"I guess I just can't stay away." I slid a quick look at Mary. "Actually, I was giving Officer Oliva some information about the Milton Gibson case."

A humorous look came into Jerry's eyes. It was the kind of look you would see a parent give a child who talks about Santa Claus. "What could you possibly have that would help our investigations? We have officers working on the case."

He didn't seem to include Mary.

"I'm aware of that, and that's why I'm bringing it to your department's attention."

He drew his lips into a line, the corners of his mouth turning upward. "You're bringing it to the attention of our file clerk. If you have information pertinent to the case, that would go to the detective in charge."

Mary stepped forward. "Yes, I was just about to give her that detective's name. Dot and I are good friends, and she felt more comfortable talking to me. The most important part of solving a crime is getting the witnesses to feel comfortable and to trust the officer, don't you agree?"

He frowned. "Absolutely, Officer O-liv-a." I wasn't sure I liked the way he pronounced her last name, putting stress on each syllable.

"Well," he said, stepping over to the sign-in log. "You need to talk to Detective Sprague, and I'm afraid he's not in the office right now. Maybe you should stop back later."

I had experienced Jerry putting me off before. This time, though, he would not stop me. "That's fine. I think I said all I need to say right now." I turned my gaze from Officer Jerry to Mary. "Besides, I'm going to be busy looking for a job. Do you have any openings here?"

Mary's eyes widened. "Looking for a job? What's wrong with the one you have now?"

"I'm back on the market."

Jerry leaned forward as if he were about to let me in on a big secret. "Maybe it's because you spend too much time playing Nancy Drew."

I leaned right back. "Maybe it's because I spend too much time helping the police see things that are right in front of their noses."

Chapter Nineteen

A day later, I pulled into the park in downtown Camden. I kept telling myself I was lucky to have found a temporary job over the holidays. There was a slight frosting of snow on the street, and as I climbed out of the car, my black boots jingled as I crossed the sidewalk to Clancy's Department Store. It also didn't help I was wearing a short green skirt with a red furry hem, red and white striped tights, a black belt, buttons that looked like peppermint candy, and more jingles on an elf hat. I tried to keep my gaze forward, even though several children and a few men leered at me. This was temporary, I kept reminding myself. Only temporary. I would continue to look for work, but until then, I'd take pictures of kids on Santa's lap. I could do this. As I opened the door, I heard a wolf whistle behind me. I turned before I could stop myself. Elwood Kirk was standing on the sidewalk in front of the barbershop.

"Aren't you the cutest little thing? If I'd known you had legs like that, I might not have given you so much grief. Jingle a little for me, honey." Elwood was partially responsible for getting me fired from my last job. There was no way I would let him get away with it twice.

"I only jingle for good little boys. Not sneaky people like you."

Elwood's face turned a deep red. It was obvious few people stood up to his bullying. He stepped forward, but before he could lay a hand on me, I escaped through the open glass door. With a smile on my face, I reported to Santa's throne. That little exchange with Elwood kept me in a good mood all morning through the tears, temper tantrums, and indignant mothers. I was leaning over the tripod, changing the film in my camera, when I heard another whistle behind me. If Elwood was back, I'd really put him on the naughty list.

"My, my. Dot Morgan. I have to say, you look stunning in that getup." Ben assessed me with a look I couldn't quite identify. He looked amused, but there was something more to it.

"Are you here to see Santa? Because he's out feeding the reindeer."

Ben snapped his fingers. "Darn, I miss him every time. Now I'll never get that train set." He stepped closer, making my heart speed up. "Maybe you could get a message to him."

"No problem. Was that the deluxe train or the one-stop special?"

"Deluxe, of course."

"Ben, I know you're not here to see Clancy's Department Store Santa. Are you following me?"

"I'll follow someone sitting on a story, but no, madam. We are together by happenstance. I'm here to pick up a gift for my nephew. He wants a G.I. Joe, complete with footlocker."

"You'd better pick it up today. I've heard several little boys ask for the same thing."

"I heard you lost your job, and believe me, I was going to check on you, but I've been busy trying to get more on the Gibson Construction story."

I was relieved to be out of that world and wasn't sure I wanted to hear what Ben had to say. All I had to worry about was keeping the kids in line and watching out for an occasional pinch from a father. "I've turned over everything I had to the police and decided to let them handle it."

"Don't you want to know what really happened? I mean, come on, Dot. We might be looking at two murders here."

Ben was right, but didn't he see what it had done to me? "I lost my job over this, Ben. Now I have to go into interviews and tell my prospective employer that Jimmy fired me from my last job because I slowed down production."

Ben wrinkled his nose. "That's what you tell them? You can think of something better than that. Tell them Gibson Construction laid you off because of a winter slowdown. That happens a lot in the construction business. Don't discount yourself. From what I could see of your work, you were an exceptionally good secretary. You went out of your way to get a second electric permit. Heck, you even brought the city clerk donuts."

"That was because it was my father, and you know it."

"Fine, but just because Jimmy labeled you as the reason for a slowdown doesn't mean you have to accept it. Why did he really fire you?"

"Because I found that bone fragment which caused the police to come out and scour the area for evidence."

"Exactly."

"Have you heard anything more about that?"

Ben leaned closer, a look of concern on his face. "You haven't been talking to Mary?"

"Not really. I've been pretty closed off. This first job was important to me, and I screwed it up. I needed time to think about my next move. She called, but I told her I'd call her back later."

"Did you?"

"Not yet."

"Fine, well, I'll tell you all I know. I need you to keep it to yourself because we don't have permission to put this in the paper yet. They found another bone out there. It looks like a hip. The hip of an older woman because it was so delicate. They can't be completely sure, but that's what they told me."

"Do they know who it is?"

"They have some ideas about the identity but didn't choose to share them with the press. Can you believe it?"

A group of children lined up behind Ben. Santa was due back from lunch in the next minute. There was a "Ho Ho Ho" behind them as Santa entered, his weary eyes on the line of wiggling children. He looked toward Ben and spoke in a low voice. "Scram, buddy. Time to get the snot parade going."

Ben nodded and moved out of the way. "Well, now that I know where you are, or rather where you can't avoid me, I'll stop back by when I know more."

I held up one finger to get Ben to wait. I led a large boy with a brown striped shirt under a corduroy coat up to Santa. Normally, I would help lift the child, but that wasn't happening. Santa patted his knee, and the boy found his way himself. "Hello there, young fella…."

I turned back to Ben. "I'm not sure if I want to know any more about these deaths."

"Sure, you do. You are as much a victim in this as Milton was. There is something rotten at Gibson Construction. Think of it this way. When you go to future job interviews, you can tell them you slowed down your last employer, or they can know all about it after reading how you exposed the truth." Ben tipped his fedora down slightly. "Along with an incredibly handsome member of the press."

Chapter Twenty

The next morning, I decided to put off the peppermint-striped tights as long as I could. I was saved when the phone rang. Ellie, usually an early riser, was still sleeping. She had been going into the dress shop later and later these days, still rambling on about the Peace Corps. Piles of dresses sat waiting for hems and adjustments, and if this kept up, she would have to either hire someone to help her or ask me to thread a needle. I was not much of a seamstress compared to Ellie. I got an A in home economics class, but all we made was a straight shift with no sleeves. Ellie made dresses with whalebone bodices and pleats.

I made it to the phone on the third ring.

Mary Oliva sounded out of breath on the other side of the line. "You're not going to believe this, but we just found another body."

Balancing the phone on my shoulder, I reached for the percolator to fill it with water. "Are you kidding? That's amazing. Anybody I know?"

"Oh yes. You know him. We found Elwood Kirk in an alley behind the Trail's End bar. It looks like maybe he got into a fight with another patron."

That was no surprise. I'd wanted to slug him myself a few times. Elwood was one of those people who had to pick at something. The kind of man who spots a weakness in another and can't stop bringing it up. Elwood Kirk was what some would call a good-looking man, but there was a layer of grime on him that would never come off.

I put the lid on the percolator and blew out a sigh. "I hate to say it, but I'm a little comforted because his death is pretty cut and dried. No intrigue, just Elwood provoking someone at a bar."

"Yeah. I guess all's right with the world. Come on, Dot. I know you never liked Elwood, and you had every right not to, but the poor man was beaten to death." As Mary scolded, I felt ashamed of myself. I never would have been this cold and callous before I worked at Gibson Construction. Was it the job, or was this just another layer of hardening after seeing John Kennedy assassinated?

"Sorry. You're right. As difficult as Elwood was, he was still somebody's son, and he did have a wife."

"The thing that bothers me about his death is I was thinking he might have been the one to kill Milton. Or he could have been the man arguing with Milton at the diner."

"What's to say he wasn't the man at the diner and the man who murdered Milton? Maybe this bar fight was an isolated incident, and someone killed our killer?"

"Maybe. Will you be around today?"

"Not until this evening. I'll be taking pictures with Santa, remember?"

Mary laughed. "Oh yeah. I forgot about that. I need to get the kids over there to get their picture. Then I want to take one myself."

"We frown upon parents taking their own pictures. Then the store doesn't make any money."

"Silly. I don't want to take a picture of them. I want to take a picture of you! Years from now, you'll thank me when you see how cute you are in that little elf outfit."

"Years from now, I'll find the picture and burn it." I laughed.

I heard the murmur of a small voice in the background. "I have to get the kids to school, but I just wanted to let you know," Mary said.

I hung up and knew it was time to pull on the tights. They were heavy material and radiated heat, made worse when surrounded by mobs of two-foot-tall people. With only one pair to go with the costume, I had carefully washed them in the sink and hung them over the shower rail to dry. This morning they were mostly dry except in the waistband. I would have to put up with it and get into work, anyway. With the overcast sky and the temperature rising, we were expecting more rain than snow. I grabbed my raincoat, grateful it would cover most of the costume.

As I drove to the department store, I glanced at the alley next to the Trail's End bar. A single patrolman stood near the back door of the bar. Ben was there, too, deep in conversation. I was already late, but yesterday we didn't have any children until at least a half hour into the shift. I parked and walked up to the men.

Ben turned and touched the edge of his hat. "Well, if it isn't Santa's elf."

The patrolman was a rookie I recognized. Mary had complained that he was already getting to do more than they allowed her to. He tipped the brim of his hat to me. "How do you do, ma'am?"

"Good morning. What happened?" I already knew the answer, but maybe this police officer might give me a little more information.

"A fight. Guy got killed back here. They just took away the body. They posted me here to make sure there isn't anybody disturbing the crime scene."

"Did you hear what the fight was about?"

"Not much. It was a pretty rowdy night at the bar, and it could have been anything."

Ben stepped in. "Do they have any idea who might have done this? I saw the victim, and it was pretty bad."

"Yeah," the cop said. "Lot of anger there. No suspects named right now."

"That means," I said, "it was probably somebody who knew Elwood."

"You knew the victim? Why would you say that?" asked the rookie.

"Because I used to work with the man, and he walked around with a chip on his shoulder."

Something about the young police officer changed. His hand strayed to his gun belt, as if ready to take down a woman in an elf costume. "And who are you?"

I would be late for work if I didn't shut up. I backed up and gave him my best casual wave. "Santa's elf, of course."

My boss, Mr. Clancy, was not too pleased when I showed up fifteen minutes late. There were three children already in line. I wasn't too concerned—this was a temporary job and not one I was planning to include on my resume.

Santa Claus didn't seem to mind, though, and had used the time to catch up on his *Reader's Digest*. I hoped he would not try to entertain me with some jokes from the "Laughter is the Best Medicine" section. I threw off my raincoat and pulled my camera and tripod out from behind Santa's throne.

I realized my exchange with the police officer could make me a suspect in Elwood's murder. It wouldn't take the police too long, though, to realize I couldn't physically have inflicted those injuries on Elwood. But a person could be beaten to death with other things besides fists. Had Elwood crossed the wrong person in the bar, or was his killer somebody who knew him? The police wouldn't find just one suspect but a line going around the corner of the police station. Elwood enjoyed bothering people, and apparently, one person decided they would not take it anymore.

Even though I was no longer directly connected to Gibson Construction, Ben was right. I needed to clear my own personal work history and prove that the problem at Gibson Construction wasn't me, but something evil. It made me shiver to think how close I had been to it, but the problem was, I had no idea what was happening when it was happening. I had been sure Elwood had killed Milton, and who was to say he didn't? But then, who killed Elwood, and why?

"Smile," I said to a tiny boy with sticky red lips. He didn't even hear me because he was too busy checking the authenticity of Santa's beard. With the flash of the bulb, I realized where I needed to go next.

Chapter Twenty-One

When I came home from another tiring day at the department store, Arlene called up the stairs. "Dot, your mother called and wants to get that necklace from you for the historical exhibit at the library. She says to call her back tonight whenever you get home."

I had forgotten about the promise to my mother about the necklace. I would have to ask Jimmy where he took it to be repaired. Talking to Jimmy about anything right now made me nervous.

I called my mother back and told her about the necklace. "Oh, that is unfortunate. You see, I told the library committee about it, and they were going to feature it as the premier piece. It is a Rasmussen, signed and everything. Can you get it back?"

"I don't know, Mom. Maybe the library ladies can put something else in the showcase."

"There's always Clara's ring she claims was worn by Judy Garland. Frankly, I don't believe her, and neither does anybody else. I mean, not to be rude, but when was she rubbing elbows with Judy Garland?"

"Perhaps on the yellow brick road?"

Mother chuckled. "I know the last thing you want to do is call the man who fired you but think of it as doing me a huge favor."

I groaned as I hung up the phone.

Chapter Twenty-Two

The next morning, on my way to work, I stopped in at Gibson Construction. The young woman behind the desk was new to me, and she resembled a deer caught unaware. "Hi, is Jimmy in?" I asked.

The young woman raised her eyebrows as I realized how the red peppermint tights must look sticking out from under my coat. "Did you have an appointment?"

"Not really. I used to do your job. In fact, I'm the one you replaced."

She raised her chin slightly, still looking unsure. "I see."

This girl exhibited all the symptoms of a Jimmy Gibson victim. I wanted to reassure her, but my elf outfit didn't quite lend credibility. "Don't worry about Jimmy. He yells a lot, but most of the time, he's in and out of the office, so you'll get some quiet time."

She let out a breath and clutched her hand to her throat. "Thank goodness. I just graduated from the Hudson Secretarial School and, well, I never imagined my boss would have such a temper. I forgot to put the date on something, and I thought he was going to fire me, you know? I don't know how you stood it." She stood to shake my hand, but the door opened, and she quickly withdrew her hand and sat back down in her chair.

"What do we have here, Lisa?" Jimmy asked.

I turned around. "Hi, Jimmy."

Jimmy let out a guffaw. "Oh my, how the mighty have fallen!"

I didn't enjoy working for the man, and now that he stood there laughing at me, I downright hated even being in his presence. "I need to know where

118

you took my necklace to be repaired. The library wants to feature it in a new exhibit. Apparently, it has some historical significance."

Jimmy's smile flattened. "Technically, that was never your necklace. It was found on Gibson property, so rightfully, it belongs to me."

"You threw it in the trash."

"And technically, that was also Gibson property."

"Finders, keepers, Jimmy. Where did you take it to be repaired?"

Jimmy turned from me to Lisa. "Did you get those purchase orders finished? We're rolling at the site and don't want to run out of materials."

"Yes, sir." Lisa handed Jimmy a stack of neatly typed forms.

"Jimmy? I need my necklace back."

"Tell it to the judge," Jimmy said as he walked out the door.

"Damn that man!" I yelled. It was obvious the gloves were off, and Jimmy wasn't even trying to be nice. I would have to call my mother and tell her Jimmy wasn't giving up the necklace. Maybe he figured out it was worth something and kept it for himself. I wouldn't put it past him.

"I'm sorry," Lisa said from behind me.

"It's not your fault." Anger seeped from every pore in my skin. Once again, Jimmy Gibson had gotten away with bullying. He bullied Milton and now me. Keeping the necklace was unfair, but legally, he was correct. It was on Gibson property, and it wouldn't be worth it to take him to court over a found necklace.

"I probably shouldn't do this." Lisa stood again.

"What?"

Lisa walked over to Jimmy's desk and opened the middle drawer. "I was looking for stamps and saw it. Or at least I think this might be it." She held up my necklace, the clasp still broken. "Take it."

As she handed it to me, I worried. "What will you say when Jimmy finds it missing?"

"That's easy. I'll tell him you found it."

"I suppose that's fair, but you don't have to do this. You don't need to get mixed up in this, not if you want to keep that job."

She bit her bottom lip. "I'm still thinking about that, too. It's my first real job, but yesterday I went home in tears."

"Makes you re-evaluate the whole situation, doesn't it?"

"You bet it does. I've been seriously thinking about changing careers. Going to beauty school. At least I'd get tips for the abuse."

I thanked Lisa and pocketed the necklace. As I headed into work, I couldn't get over how much happier I was now that I no longer worked for Gibson Construction. Sure, I had to deal with crying, impatient children all day, but even the most tempestuous toddler wasn't as bad as Jimmy Gibson.

I walked over to the library at my lunchtime and gave my mother the necklace.

"He gave it back. Very good. Maybe he isn't such a monster."

"He didn't give it back to me. He refused. He said I found it on Gibson property, so technically it was his."

My mother's eyebrows rose, causing a row of wrinkles to dance up her forehead. "If he didn't give it to you, then how did you get it?"

"It was in his desk drawer, and the new secretary gave it to me after he left." I had never met this girl in secretarial school, but now I wished I had. I admired her for recognizing Gibson Construction as a hostile environment on only her second day. I could also relate to not wanting to quit her first job out of secretarial school.

"Oh my. This is getting interesting. He seemed like such a nice man when you first talked about him, then things changed, I guess. Didn't you tell me you fished the necklace out of the trash?"

"Yes."

"Well, anything thrown away is no longer that person's possession. Everyone knows that."

"And then he took it away and tossed it in his drawer. You know, he sure is concerned about that necklace. It makes me wonder why."

Mother set aside her overdue book file and bit her bottom lip in thought. "That is strange. Do you think he's greedy on principle, or is it something else?"

"I'm not sure. But I do have an idea. When do you have to have the necklace?"

"The exhibit starts in two days. I almost never see your boss in the library, so I doubt he'll even know we have it."

I held out my hand. "Okay, I should have it back to you by tomorrow. Does that sound good?"

"Sure. I never wanted to feature Judy Garland's ring, anyway."

Ellie poked her head around a book stack. "I thought I recognized that voice."

I looked at the clock on the wall. "Did you close the store for lunch?"

"I put the store on Christmas vacation. It's about time I took one. Did you know that you can go for miles in Africa without modern conveniences? It's like living in another century."

"With the bonus of bugs and malaria," my mother added.

Ellie slipped her a caustic look. "They have bugs here. Come on, Aunt Opal, I think you, of all people, would be supportive of me going. You're always talking about exploring new worlds."

"In books. I meant in books. Ellie, you have a thriving business that you've built with your own talent. How can you even think of leaving that behind? Besides that, what about Al? Men like that don't come along every day."

Ellie slammed a large, heavy tome about Africa on the counter, making the overdue card tray shake. "What you're really saying is I may not get another chance because instead of looking like Cinderella, like your daughter, I turned out like an ugly stepsister. Isn't that it? You're both afraid if I leave now, I'll end up an old maid?"

The thought had crossed my mind, but I didn't dare say it. "We're worried about you, Ellie," I said in a much quieter voice.

Ellie signed the library card. "Well, don't. I'm doing just fine. In a way, the assassination experience was good for me. I've realized life is short, and if I don't start living it, then it's nobody's fault but my own." She pushed the signed card across the counter. "It's almost one, Dot. You'd better get back to the store."

"I still have ten minutes," I answered.

Mother turned to Ellie. "I need to call your mother. She has to be beside herself with what's going on."

Ellie picked up her book and turned to leave. "She's fine. I'm fine. We're all fine. You worry too much, Aunt Opal."

I watched my cousin while feeling the tiredness seeping into my jingly black boots. "I wish we'd never gone to see President Kennedy in Dallas. Once you see something like that, it stays with you. It's like a little worm eating away your insides, and you can't make it stop."

My mother's gaze went from Ellie to me. "I hope that doesn't mean you're planning on doing something rash?"

"No, but it affected how I felt about my new job. I'm not sure if I really want to be a secretary."

Ellie gave me a knowing nod.

A gentle grin came across her face. "That's because you're a smart girl. Nobody says just because you have office skills, you have to use them to make some man's coffee. Have you thought about applying somewhere that can really use all you have to offer?"

I felt relief in my mother's reaction. My parents had helped pay for secretarial school and my living arrangement with Ellie. I felt guilty for hating the daily drudgery of the job. Filing, answering the phone, typing, trying not to make mistakes. Then there was the matter of the clock. When I was outside of work, my time flew. I never had enough of it. When I was sitting behind the desk at Gibson Construction, I watched the minutes tick by slowly.

"What am I going to do?" I felt myself getting more emotional. All the doubts I'd been pushing away now came to the surface.

"Follow your heart. That's all you can do. Just remember, you're not locked into anything. You don't have to be a secretary. You don't even have to stay in Camden, although we would miss you. I kind of think there's a certain young newspaper reporter who would miss you, too."

I was amazed at her insight and how easily she was allowing me to try a new path. Was Ben noticing me? "Do you think so?"

"I know so. Trust me. You walk into a room, and he can't keep his eyes off you. His face brightens up like a new penny."

I reached over and kissed my mother's cheek. "Thanks, Mom."

CHAPTER TWENTY-TWO

"What for?"

"For being you and letting me be me."

Later that afternoon, as I worked through an endless line of children, I spotted a familiar face. Isabella stood in line with her son, Freddie. Isabella was staring into her compact mirror, her big brown eyes beautifully shaped with eyeliner and full lips painted a deep shade of red. Freddie leaned against a glass counter, looking at a set of Lincoln Logs. I tried to think of what I planned to say to Isabella, given the hostile tone of our last meeting. I didn't approve of what Isabella had done with Milton's belongings or her quick leap into a love affair with Arturo. It led me to think dark thoughts. Did Isabella feel so stymied by Milton she had him killed? Had she been the one to drug his coffee on the day of the demolition?

I didn't want to think that way because she was my friend Mary's sister-in-law, and John's sister. John was a hardworking father and husband, and I would trust him with my life. I couldn't say the same about Isabella.

"Dot? Is that you?" Isabella took in my costume. She clipped her compact closed and laughed. Freddie came up and immediately ran his fingers along the red fur at the bottom of the short skirt.

"Neato," was all he said.

"Hi, Isabella. How are you?"

"Well, obviously better than you. Is Jimmy not paying you enough over there at Gibson Construction?"

"Jimmy isn't paying me at all. He fired me."

Isabella covered a smile with her hand. Her shoulders bounced once as she stopped a laugh. "How did you get fired?"

I didn't have to answer and decided I wouldn't. "Hi, Freddie. Ready to see Santa Claus?"

Freddie motioned me closer with his hand. "Is that the real Santa Claus?"

"As real as we could get. Do you know what you want for Christmas?"

Freddie nodded, his oval brown eyes staring at Santa. "Yes, ma'am."

As twins crawled off Santa's lap, Freddie, with just a little urging, walked over to the big man in red. I focused my camera on the two while Isabella spoke quietly over her shoulder.

"I suppose you've told everyone you know that I'm with Arturo now."

I focused the lens while Freddie whispered in Santa's ear. "I don't know that many people. It's really none of my business."

Isabella's head twitched slightly. "Arturo is so different from Milton. He's going places, and he loves Freddie. He told me he wants to own this town someday. He thinks he should run Gibson Construction."

I turned away from the camera. "How is he planning to do that?"

"We are raising a Gibson grandson, now, aren't we? I hadn't even thought that far ahead, but Arturo said it's a terrific opportunity to keep it in the family. Now that we're going to become a family. He's so smart, so handsome."

So manipulative, I thought. Santa cleared his throat, and I returned to the camera. With a couple of clicks, I took Freddie's picture and gave Isabella a card with a date to pick up the pictures along with a receipt to pay at the cash register. "I don't want to be a killjoy here, but did you ever think Arturo might be more interested in Gibson Construction than he is in you and Freddie?"

Isabella's cheeks flushed. "You've become very bitter, Dot. How could you say such a thing? Arturo loves me, and he's already the most exciting man I've ever...known."

She walked over and jerked little Freddie's arm, pulling him off Santa's lap, knocking a bag of candy canes by Santa's side to the floor. I rushed over to help Santa pick them up. "Sorry about that. I think I made her angry."

Santa waved a red-mittened hand. "That's fine." Once Isabella and Freddie were out of earshot, Santa whispered, "That little boy just shared the saddest Christmas wish I've ever heard."

"What was that?"

"He wants his daddy to be alive again."

I slowed as I picked up the last candy cane and straightened just as Isabella and Freddie exited the store. My heart went out to the boy who had just lost his father, a sweet dear man. His new father wouldn't be so kind.

Chapter Twenty-Three

"There you are." My landlady, Arlene, trudged through the door. "I was hoping to talk to you earlier, but I guess they have you working long hours over at the department store."

Arlene had three cookbooks on the coffee table of her living room, an area I had to walk through to get to the upstairs. "Did you need me for something?"

"I need an opinion. You know I'm having my annual Christmas party on Friday, but this is all making me so nervous, I'm tempted to take one of my mother's little helpers. Should we have a turkey or ham as the main dish?"

"Is this going to be a sit-down dinner?"

"No, I want to do it buffet style. Something new for me this year. Whatever I cook needs to be easy to carry around on a plate."

I sat down and looked through the recipes Arlene had marked in the cookbooks. "I'd go with this." I pointed to a picture of a stack of sandwiches.

"It doesn't seem too informal?"

"Not at all. Besides, you can make it festive with Christmas cookies and cakes."

"You're right." She closed the other two cookbooks. "I hope you're planning on coming. I know you've been through a lot lately."

"I think I'm one girl who's looking forward to 1964 like nobody else. New Year. Fresh start. All that."

"Do the police know who killed Milton yet?"

"I haven't heard anything. Pardon me for asking, but just what is a mother's little helper?"

Arlene laughed. "Oh, sorry. I'm not sure if they call it that anymore. It's a pill. A tranquilizer. They prescribed them a lot in the fifties. Take too many, and they make you loopy. Take them too long, and you can't stop taking them. One of my friends had a devil of a time stopping. Anyway, they gave them out like candy to women overwhelmed with the kiddies, the house, the hubby. You know."

"Do they still prescribe them?"

"Sure, some doctors do, although not like they used to."

I thought about the clumps in the coffee. "What color were the pills?"

"Mine were yellow, although I've seen them in blue and in white. Why are you so interested? Is this new job so bad? You need one?"

"No. You're going to think this sounds silly, but I had Milton's thermos from the day of the accident. When I went to wash it out, I found yellow clumps of something in it. I collected some of it in a handkerchief."

"What are you saying? You think someone drugged Milton?"

"You should have seen him. One minute he was fine, and the next, he was walking around in a daze. That beam hit him, and he barely looked up."

Arlene looked amazed at this new information. "You need to tell the police about this." Arlene reached for the black phone on an end table.

"I already have. Well, I told Mary about it and gave her what I could collect out of the thermos with a handkerchief."

"Good. If somebody drugged Milton that day, there's a good chance they were trying to murder him."

"He recovered, and he seemed to be doing fine, but when I talked to him in the hospital, he was different."

"Someone just hit him in the head. Maybe they knocked something loose."

"It was more than that. He was frightened. Like he knew someone was trying to kill him."

"If that's the case, then why didn't he say something? Tell his wife or his family?"

I thought about the group of people Milton could have gone to for support. If I had a choice between Isabella, Jimmy, or Harry, I might clam up too.

"Well, I can help one way." Arlene rose and smoothed out her skirt. "Wait here."

A minute later, she came back with a little yellow pill in her hand. "Take this to Mary. Maybe there's a way they can compare it."

"You think so?"

"Sure. They do all kinds of things now with the wonders of modern science."

I put the pill in my pocket, feeling the necklace I had put there earlier. I had one more errand to run.

After changing into more comfortable clothes, I called the Gibson house. To my dismay, Jimmy answered.

"I was wondering if I could have a word with your father."

"Why?" Jimmy asked.

I stiffened. "I think that's between me and your father."

"He's not here."

It seemed to me that Harry was almost always at home. "Where is he?"

"Why do you care?"

I wasn't getting anywhere with this man. Listening to him bark at me made me wonder how I lasted as long as I did. "So, how's the project going? Any more slowdowns?" I asked, with a slight edge to my voice. He wasn't my boss, and I didn't have to put up with his attitude if I didn't want to. I already knew he wouldn't give me a letter of recommendation, so why not get in a jab?

"It's at a total standstill, thanks to you. And now, on top of everything else, Arturo Galvez wants to meet me out at the site tomorrow to discuss my options. What the hell is he talking about? It seems to have something to do with you."

"Did they find any more bones?"

"Why do you care? Because of you, I'm having to answer a lot of stupid questions about former renters. You should come with a warning label, Dot. Caution, this secretary will screw up your life."

"I could say the same for you, Jimmy. Tell me, just how many secretaries do you run through in a year?" I had never questioned how long the last girl was there or the one before that. If he was such a terrible boss, why hadn't the secretarial school warned me about him?

"None of your business. All you young girls are alike. You don't know the meaning of hard work. One little kerfuffle, and you lose it."

"I never lost it."

"No. You were too busy taking down the entire business."

I heard a sound in the background.

"Who's that?" the voice said.

There was a rustling as the sound became muted, probably from Jimmy's hand covering the receiver.

When he came back on, he stated succinctly, "We're not interested." He was clearly trying to make it sound as if he were dealing with a bothersome sales call. Harry Gibson was there, just as I thought, but Jimmy was running interference.

I'd have to wait until Jimmy wasn't home. I'd try again tomorrow. As I hung up the phone, I felt happy, almost giddy. It was stupid, really, but standing up to a man like that made a girl feel good.

The next morning, I got a call that Santa was down. He'd picked up a bug, most probably from one of the dear little children with green runny noses. My throat didn't seem to be affected at all, and although I'd miss the money I would have made, I was looking forward to a day off. The elf job was a straight through thing. Every day until Christmas Eve. But Santa had given us both the gift of a day off.

The first thing I wanted to do was to go by the Gibson house and see if Jimmy's car was there. If he wasn't there, I might have a chance to talk to Harry. I might also drop in on Ben to see if he'd learned anything new. I bounded out of bed with a new sense of urgency. Milton didn't have too many friends, and I wanted to do this for him. I threw on a tan cashmere turtleneck sweater and a pair of brown tweed pants.

"Where are you going?" Ellie asked as she stared at the percolator bubbling on the counter.

"Unexpected day off. I'm going to see a man about a necklace." I pulled a cup from the metal cup tree on the counter.

"What about you?" I was almost afraid to ask. Ellie was at her shop sporadically these days. I had heard her on the phone just the other day as a wedding party canceled on her.

"Al wants to take me to lunch."

"How's that going?"

"Don't ask." The percolator stopped, and Ellie poured herself a cup of the hot steaming liquid. After taking a sip, she turned to me. "Hey. You could do me a favor today."

"What's that?"

"Come to lunch with us."

I wasn't sure I wanted to be a third wheel. "I don't think Al wants to talk to me."

"Exactly. Last time we did this, he started crying, right there at the lunch counter. I can't take it again."

"I don't know."

"Please, Dot. It's either you go with me, or I cancel on Al. I can't take watching him lose it like that. It breaks my heart."

I wanted to correct her and tell her she was the one breaking his heart, but I had learned long ago that when Ellie got an idea in her head, it was best to just let her run with it.

I poured myself a cup of coffee, adding two sugar cubes to it. "I'll think about it. When and where?"

"Twelve o'clock at the lunch counter downtown. It would be great if you could. Why don't you invite Ben to come? I'm sure he'd love to see you again."

I took a sip and grinned. "Maybe."

Ellie gave me a big smile. It was the kind of smile I hadn't seen since before the assassination. Ellie peered closely. "I think Dot's in love."

"Stop. Dot's interested. That's as far as I'm willing to commit at this point."

"Given the color in your cheeks, I would say Dot is very interested."

As I knocked on the Gibsons' door an hour later, I was still thinking about my conversation with Ellie. I was very interested in Ben, but with men, I wasn't all that sure how to proceed next. I'd had boyfriends in high school, but they were more like members of the same club. There were kisses on the dance floor, and a few on the front porch, but I had never felt the desire to go any further. They were nice boys, but that was it. They were boys. Slicked back hair, bubble gum, and plans for futures that didn't involve me.

There was no answer at the door, so I tried again. Just when I decided to give up and began walking down the front porch stairs, I heard a woman's voice on the other side. "Wait a minute. Wait a minute." She slurred her words even through the door. She took forever to fumble with the locks on the other side. Each time the sound would stop, I would hear *wait a minute*, as if she were working through an intricate puzzle.

When the door finally opened, a woman in her sixties, blonde hair askew, and wearing a pink quilted bathrobe with fuzzy white mules on her feet, stood before me. "Can I help you?" she slurred.

"Mrs. Gibson?" I wasn't sure if this was Jimmy's mother, but based on descriptions I'd heard, this had to be her.

"Yeah?"

"Hi, I'm Dot Morgan. I work for...I used to work for your son, Jimmy."

Mrs. Gibson leaned against the doorway. "Jimmy's not here."

"I know." I reached into my brown suede coat pocket and extracted the necklace. "I was wondering if you could identify this. Do you know who it might have belonged to?"

Mrs. Gibson took the necklace into her pale hands. "Celeste." She brought up her bottom lip as her mouth shaped into a deep frown. "This was Celeste's. Where did you find it?"

"Milton found it."

"He did? Why didn't he tell me?"

"He didn't know whose it was. Jimmy threw it in the trash, and I pulled it out and cleaned it up."

"Why did you have to clean it up?"

"Milton found it in the dirt at the construction site."

Mrs. Gibson examined it closely, turning it around side to side, and then she held it to her heart. "Celeste."

"Where is Celeste now, if I may ask?"

CHAPTER TWENTY-THREE

"Don't know. She disappeared about a year ago. I miss her so much."

"I think I saw your picture with her when I was talking to your husband, Mrs. Gibson."

"Call me Agnes. Won't you come in?"

She stepped back, and as I entered, I worried what Jimmy would say if he found me there. "I tried to call last night to talk to your husband, but Jimmy wouldn't let me. Was your husband out last night?"

She reached up and tried to pat down her wild hair with her free hand. "I don't think so. I, uh. Have spells where I forget things."

From what I had heard, it was more than spells. "How long had you known Celeste?"

"Oh, years. We went to school together. She was my best friend. She could be stubborn, I tell you, but I loved the woman. When we were kids, we had our own tree we carved on and even a fort in the woods. Well, it was a big stone, but we called it our fort. She told me we'd always be friends and that she'd never leave me. I don't understand any of it."

"I'm sorry you haven't been able to find her."

"Yes. Some days I don't feel like getting out of bed. And some days, it's just the pills that get me through."

"Can I ask you, what color are the pills?"

The old woman looked strangely at me. "I take a lot of pills. They're all colors."

I should have thought of that. "Are any of them yellow?"

"Well, yes. Those are my settle-down pills. Those are the ones that get me through some days."

"Does anyone else have access to those pills?"

"Just me, I guess. I get them from Dr. Sanderson. You know him—the one Isabella works for. She's such a sweet girl. I don't know what she'll do now that Milton's gone. I'm not sure if she can support herself on her nurse's salary. We'll be there for her, of course, for her and little Freddie."

Agnes was not aware that her sweet daughter-in-law was about to move on with Camden's most up-and-coming entrepreneur, Arturo Galvez. When she found out, it would break her heart, and I decided I wouldn't be the one to share that news. "I'm sorry I didn't come and talk to you at the funeral."

"I wasn't there. The doctor said it would be too difficult for me, so I stayed in my room. They gave me a sedative. Harry didn't want me to have to talk to people."

"I understand."

A sob escaped Agnes's lips. "But I do miss him, you know? He was so like my father. Quiet, sweet, and a man who would always take the high road. Jimmy is like his father. He gets incredibly focused on proving to his father that he is taking care of the business. He told me once he plans to make it an enormous success and make Harry proud. That's Jimmy." Her watery eyes took me in. "But I guess you know that already."

"Sure." I rose to leave. "Thank you for your time today, and I'm sorry for your loss. The library would like to feature the necklace in an exhibit. If you let me borrow it, I'll return it right after the event is over."

She looked at the necklace for a moment and then handed it to me. "I think Celeste would love having her necklace in an exhibit. Especially if it's at the library."

"Thank you. I enjoyed working with Milton. He was always so nice to me. I'll miss him."

"Yes." She looked out the window. "There's a part of me that will never be the same. I can't imagine why Milton would have found this in the dirt. She treasured it so very much. I can't recall a time when she wasn't wearing it."

Chapter Twenty-Four

Ellie's store, Blue Bonnets, was fairly close to the Gibson home and I was bursting with my discovery. When I rushed inside and made my way through the rainbow rows of taffeta dresses, I found Ellie leaning on the counter, looking out at the red velvet Christmas dress she had made to display in the window.

It occurred to me that of all the times I had come into the store, this was the first time I'd seen Ellie standing still. She was usually waiting on a customer, steaming a dress, or sewing in the back room. Today she looked listless, her hand under her chin, her eyes fixed. "Guess what? You're never going to believe this, but—" Ellie's gaze didn't waver. "Ellie? Are you all right?"

"I'm fine," she said, as if she were taking a casual stroll in the park. Instead of buzzing around Blue Bonnets, always making it better, she was quiet. If she continued to be this inattentive, she could lose her store.

I looked around. Something didn't look right. "Don't you usually have your Christmas tree up by now? It would look great next to that red dress."

Ellie stood up and hugged herself with her long arms. "It would."

"Do you want me to help you put it up? Remember, I have the day off."

Her gaze moved to the window. "Sure. That would be great." This was a task Ellie normally loved to do. Today she sounded like she was doing the dishes, not ringing in the season.

I waited, but Ellie had become quiet again. "So? Where are the boxes of Christmas decorations?" Ellie usually put up an aluminum Christmas tree with shiny ornaments. Hers had a little wheel attached to a light that she placed on the floor under the tree. As the colors on the wheel changed, so did the tint on the tree.

"Oh," Ellie pulled her gaze away. "Um, in the back room on the top shelf. I'll get them. Watch the front for me, okay?"

"Sure." It wasn't like there was any foot traffic. Ellie was in a funk, and by now, the rest of the town knew it. There were probably bets down at the VFW hall how long she would stay open past January. Ellie was making a mistake. I needed to talk some sense into her.

I walked over to the window to clear space for the tree next to the red velvet dress that had been put over Dolly, Ellie's window mannequin. Al's truck pulled up in front.

He came through the door like he was on his way to put out a fire. "Where's Ellie?"

"I'm not sure if she wants to speak with you, Al. Besides, weren't we supposed to be meeting for lunch today?"

"This couldn't wait," Al said.

Ellie walked through the curtain that separated the front from the back of the store. "She's right. I don't feel like talking to you. I was about to call you to cancel lunch, but to do that, I would have to talk to you."

Al threw his hands up in the air. "You keep putting me off."

Ellie straightened her dress catalogs on the counter. "Sorry. I've been busy."

I felt like melting into the dress rack. "I'll just step outside for a minute. "

"Don't you go anywhere," Ellie bellowed. "It's your fault for letting him in the door to begin with." I stayed, placing my hands at my side.

"So, are you busy or just too busy to talk to me? What's going on here, Ellie? I think I've given you more than enough time to get over this thing."

"And that is exactly the problem between the two of us, Al. You're waiting for me to get over something. My dream doesn't matter to you."

Al drew closer. "Of course, what you want matters to me. That's why I asked you to marry me, but honestly, Ellie, how am I supposed to deal with this?"

Ellie put her fists to her mouth and squeezed her eyes shut. "I don't know, Al. I don't know anything anymore."

"This is a direct reaction to what you saw in Dallas. I get that. The world is a rotten evil place, but that doesn't mean you have to go off to some foreign country to make it better. Ellie, I want you to stay here."

Ellie's lips drew into a line. "It's all about what Al wants, never about what Ellie wants. I guess I shouldn't have expected you to understand how I'm feeling. I thought a lot about this." She paused for a moment. "I'm calling the engagement off." She slipped the diamond ring off her finger and set it on the counter. "Sometimes we outgrow people, Al, and I've outgrown you."

Al stared down at the ring on the glass countertop. He looked back up at Ellie. "No. You don't mean that. You're just going through a troubled time. You don't mean that."

"Indeed, I do. I need you to be on your way. Take your ring and go. We have a lot to do in the store today, right, Dot?"

I had felt invisible while they talked, but I gave her a quick nod.

Al continued to stare at the ring. "Keep it. I can't make you do things, so I guess it's only fair you can't make me take it. Besides, I'm not planning to ask anybody else to marry me." Al slammed the door on the way out, causing the bells to bang against the glass. Ellie followed him with her eyes. Al opened his truck door and then slammed it as he settled himself into the seat.

"You shouldn't have done that," I said in a whisper. For the first time, I noticed Ellie's eyes filled with tears.

"Probably not. I just can't have Al in the way right now. Can't you understand that? Why can't anybody understand that?"

I did understand on one level. Our day in Dallas had also influenced me because I was rethinking my own career choices. But Ellie had a successful business and a kind man she loved and had finally convinced him to marry her. She was giving it all up because of that one split second.

For the next hour, I tried to get Ellie to talk about Al, but my cousin went through putting up the tree like she was a machine. Every answer was monosyllabic, and she rarely looked up and made eye contact. I tried to tell Ellie about the necklace, but in the middle of my story, she went into the backroom for something. Ellie wasn't listening to anything I had to say. Once I finished helping put up Ellie's tree, I was still bursting with my news and needed to tell someone. Who else would get this excited? Ben. I turned the corner and walked over to the *Camden Courier* offices.

"Dot, what a surprise. No little kids to wrangle today?"

"Nope, I have the day off. Santa's sick." I told Ben about my meeting with Agnes.

"You're saying the necklace belongs to Mrs. Gibson's best friend? This is news."

"Yes, it is, and we need to take this information to the police."

Ben gave a playful smile. "Or we could try to figure out the case ourselves, and I would have the most incredible story in the *Camden Courier* this year. I might even get the Pulitzer."

"Don't you think this is a little dangerous to try and solve this case on our own? At least the police carry guns."

"I don't need to carry a gun. I carry the pen of journalism."

I wasn't so sure that Ben's pen would be a good defense against a murderer. "Still, I think we should tell the police about this."

Ben put both of his hands together in a praying position. "Just give me a little more time. Please?"

It would be good to have more figured out before Officer Jerry, and his kind shut down the information on the case. "Okay. Let's talk about this. Who would want Celeste dead?"

Ben snapped his fingers in the air. "Gibson Construction would."

"I'm not sure. I thought all the people in the rental houses had been glad to leave, besides Jimmy owned the last rental house."

"You mean Jimmy was Celeste's landlord?"

"Yeah, but he never mentioned having any trouble with her moving out."

"Who else?"

I thought back to my conversation with Harry. "She was best friends with Agnes. I think Harry was jealous of their friendship. They spent a lot of time together. Harry seems like he was very possessive of his wife, and he wasn't too happy with the idea of sharing her."

"Okay, we have Harry, or we have Jimmy. Which one would have the biggest reason to murder Celeste?"

CHAPTER TWENTY-FOUR

"That is, if Celeste was even under that house. We're making an assumption."

I was sure it had to be Celeste but agreed anyway. "You're right. But who else could it be? I found her necklace, and then we found a piece of bone, and the police found even more."

"But we don't know if it's her bone." Ben put a hand to his chin in thought.

A thought came to me. "The excavator."

Ben took a sip of his coffee and grimaced. "Lukewarm. What about the excavator?"

"Somebody dumped it in the pit. We never found out who it was. Could it be that Harry went out to dig up the body and dumped it in the hole because he didn't know how to operate a newer piece of machinery like that?"

"Seems to me once you drive one excavator, you've driven them all," Ben said.

"Sure, but if you hadn't done it in years, you might forget things. Right?"

"I suppose. He is pretty old."

The more I thought of it, the more it seemed to fit together. "He isn't too old to kill someone. I think I need to talk to Harry again."

Ben sat up. "Not without me."

"Or we could do the sensible thing and turn all of this over to the police."

"One day. Then we tell them. It's my career at stake."

"We could get a look at the police file. The pictures should be back from the developer by now."

Ben scratched his head. "And how are we going to do that?"

Mary's face came to mind. "I have a friend who has the exquisite opportunity to file everything."

"Yeah. But what if it's on a detective's desk?"

I winked. "Leave it to me. I'll bet we could get our hands on that file."

Mary called that evening, her voice in a whisper. "Detective Sprague has gone home for the day. If you're going to do it, now is the time."

"I just have to call Ben, but I'll be right over."

"No, Ben. I don't want the press involved in this. I know you think he's a great guy, but if he's a reporter, I don't trust him. Call him and tell him you'll give him a full report, but I don't want him in here with our files. I'd get fired."

After breaking the news to a disappointed Ben, I was at the police station ten minutes later. Mary met me in the front lobby. A curious rookie cop behind the desk looked up as we passed. Mary gave him a nod, and he returned to his paperwork. As we stepped into the detective's room, now empty, Mary walked me to Sprague's desk. He had stacked all his files on the right-hand side, and his green-marbled desk blotter was empty. Sprague was neat. Everything in its place. A good habit to have if your job was putting together clues to a murder. Mary pulled a file out of the stack. She looked to the door, and then motioned to me to pull up a chair.

We began with pictures of Milton, brutally slain, parts of his skull caved in. "Do they know what hit him?" I asked.

"Let me look at the coroner's report."

After flipping through several sheets of paper, she slowed, and then pointed to a paragraph on the page. "It says here that the break in the skull left a circular mark. It was round, and they think it could've possibly been a hammer or some other hand tool with a round base."

"What about the waitresses' eyewitness reports?"

"Here they are." Mary handed me a piece of paper. "You read this one, and I'll read the other one."

I quickly read through the eyewitness account but learned nothing new. Two men arguing out on the curb, hard to see. One was taller than the other, and the witness couldn't hear what they were quarreling about, but it was a heated argument.

"It would be so much easier if we knew what they were arguing about."

"Nope. Nobody knows, but my money is it has something to do with the body they found behind the house."

I shook my head and turned the autopsy photo face down. "Do you think Milton knew something?"

"Unfortunately for him, I think he did. He's the one who found the necklace. How long did it take him to go from the necklace to who it belonged to? Either he figured it out or whoever killed him thought he knew more than he did." Mary returned to reading her witness statement.

She pointed to the height of the second man. "Who is the tallest man in the Gibson family?"

"I'm not sure."

"Well, whoever it was, they were taller than Milton."

"What about Arturo Galvez? He's taller than Milton, isn't he?" I asked.

"Yes, he is. Which reminds me, Isabella finally told John that Arturo was moving in with her and little Freddie."

"Without being married and so soon after Milton's death? How did John take that?"

Mary curled her lip into a scowl. "How do you think? He doesn't like it at all. He doesn't trust Arturo, and he thinks he's using Isabella for her connection to the Gibson money."

"I think the same. As long as she has little Freddie, she has a tie to the Gibsons, and he knows that."

Mary leaned back in Detective Sprague's chair. "Arturo is an ambitious man, but is he so ambitious he would kill Milton to get to Isabella?"

"And the money, an heir to the Gibson fortune, could bring to him. Maybe."

"Who should we question first?" Mary asked.

"I already spoke with Harry. He admits he was jealous but didn't have any idea about the necklace. I've never heard of a husband killing another woman out of jealousy."

"I have female friends, and my husband isn't so jealous that he sets out to kill them. Or has John been threatening you?"

I laughed at her suggestion. "No, he's been perfectly nice to me. Somehow, these deaths relate to each other. They must. The bones at the strip mall site. Milton. And then Elwood Kirk. He's taller than Milton, too."

"Are you sure that Elwood's death isn't because he is such a horse's ass?"

I let out a sigh. It had been a long day, and it felt like we were going around in circles. "Possibly." I handed back her witness statement. "But for now, I feel like they connect. I still need to tell Ben about my conversation with Harry."

"Are you sure about that? What if he writes about it and interferes with the police investigation?"

"He promised me he wouldn't."

Mary crossed her arms and didn't look like she believed me. "Right."

Chapter Twenty-Five

U nfortunately, the next day Santa checked in with a clean bill of health, and I was back to taking pictures of anxious toddlers. I had to admit this job wasn't too bad. My boss wasn't yelling at me for no reason, and the kids were cute. All I could see was hope in so many little eyes. Christmas did that. No matter what kinds of lousy things were going on in the world, Santa Claus, Christmas trees, candy canes, and hope made it better. This was one moment when I knew I was in the right place for me. Santa wasn't too bad to deal with, even if he complained constantly, but I had to consider he spent his day listening to a slew of demands. He had a right to vent a little.

When we'd made it through the line of children, Santa decided to step out for a smoke break. I was cleaning up candy wrappers when the store owner, Mr. Clancy, walked over and asked me to come to the office. I followed him upstairs to the small office that overlooked the sales floor. Jimmy Gibson stood inside the door, his arms crossed and his foot tapping.

Mr. Clancy nodded to Jimmy. "Mr. Gibson, here, came to me with a complaint about you. He tells me you have a possession of his."

Just when I was having a good day. "Mr. Gibson knows when you throw something away, it is legally the property of whoever takes it out of the trash," I said.

Jimmy cleared his throat and exchanged glances with Mr. Clancy and another man in the room. "That necklace being in the trash can was a mistake. It fell in by accident," Jimmy said.

"Well then, I guess that's something for a judge to decide because you told me it was trash and to throw it away."

Jimmy's face was unreadable, making me think of a grand master at chess, making his next move. "It's your word against mine, isn't it? The point is, we found the necklace on Gibson property, and it belongs to me. My mother was babbling about it last night. And by the way, who do you think you are, agitating a woman who is clearly not within her own senses? It took us all night to settle her down. She couldn't stop talking about that friend of hers. If I hadn't fired you already, I certainly would fire you immediately." He turned to my new boss. "Let me give you a piece of advice. Don't let this one out of your sight. You might find some inventory missing."

Mr. Clancy's eyebrows rose slightly at the suggestion. "We keep a careful eye on all our employees. But this woman has done nothing to raise suspicion. The children and parents all seem to love her."

I didn't expect my new boss to stand up for me. Maybe all bosses weren't like Jimmy Gibson after all. This not only made me happy at this moment but gave me hope.

Jimmy's eyebrows rose slightly, then he made a *tsking* sound. "Maybe not, but if I were you, I'd start taking inventory of what's on that sales floor before something disappears."

I couldn't stand listening to Jimmy's accusations another minute, and jumped in. "I didn't steal the necklace, and I don't plan to steal from Clancy's, and I'm insulted you would even suggest anything like that."

Mr. Clancy raised a finger and wagged at the both of us. "We take security very seriously, Mr. Gibson, I assure you. As I said, Miss Morgan has given us no cause for concern, but since she is a new, and temporary, employee, a bit of extra caution might be prudent. Miss Morgan, just check in with me before you leave each evening."

His solution was like a slap in the face, and Jimmy's wide grin reminded me of the Cheshire Cat from *Alice in Wonderland*. "Glad to hear it, old man." He turned to me. "I'm going to have to take this matter up with the police. You haven't heard the last of me yet. You'll be sorry for the day you crossed Jimmy Gibson and the Gibson family."

Once dismissed, I returned to my station behind the camera, but Jimmy's words echoed in my ears. I was sure he'd follow through on his threat and go to the police over the necklace. Sure enough, a policeman showed up within the hour and asked me to come to the station and answer a few questions about a missing piece of jewelry.

As I took my seat behind a plain, vanilla-colored interview table, I couldn't help but notice the hum of the overhead light. My elf shoes made a jingling sound as I settled into the chair.

Detective Sprague sat across the table from me, playing with the corner of his mustache. He smiled. "Nice to see you again, Dot. All right, tell me what happened to the necklace." I knew Detective Sprague from a case he worked last year, and I liked him. If anyone would listen to my side, it was him.

"Listen, I don't know what Jimmy Gibson told you, but this all started when he threw the necklace in the trash."

"Anybody else but you see or hear this?" Sprague asked.

"There was another person in the room, but unfortunately, he's not talking. Milton Gibson, his brother, was there."

"That's too bad for you, Dot. I'm afraid that if Mr. Gibson takes this to court, it'll be a case of who is the most believable. Tell me, if you were on the jury, who would you believe? The head of Gibson Construction or a novice secretary in her first job?"

When he put it that way, it seemed there was no way I would win. The best thing I could do would be to give the necklace back to Jimmy. "Did Mr. Gibson tell you his mother recognized the necklace?"

Sprague had been writing on a piece of paper, but then his small gray eyes looked up at me. "Do tell."

"Agnes Gibson said it belonged to a woman named Celeste. She was a lifelong friend of Agnes, who last year disappeared without a trace. Agnes was heartbroken over her friend's disappearance, and when she saw the necklace, I'm afraid it riled her up. That's part of the reason Jimmy was so upset about the necklace resurfacing and being in my possession again."

Detective Sprague tapped his index finger on the table. "Celeste Wilson?"

I pulled the necklace out of my pocket and handed it to Sprague. "Yes. All I know is this necklace belonged to Celeste, and Agnes immediately recognized it."

"If I could get you to hold on here for just a minute, I'll be right back. Don't go anywhere."

I shuffled slightly as the detective rose. A minute later, he returned with a manila file in his hands. "Celeste Wilson. We have a file on her. I'm finding this very interesting. If you don't mind, I'd like you to leave the necklace here with the police."

I thought of my mother's exhibit at the library but knew she would bow to the wishes of the police. "I guess so."

"Thank you, and thank you for telling us about the owner of the necklace. That's all we need for now. We'll call you if we have any more questions."

I had the rest of the day off, so I headed home to change and then stopped by the *Camden Courier* to see if Ben was at work. I had a lot of facts rolling around in my mind, and I hoped he would help me sort them out. His eyes lit up as he spotted me across the crowded newsroom through the clouds of cigarette smoke.

"Well, this is a surprise. What brings you here today? I was thinking about calling you, but you saved me a step."

"I just came from being questioned by the police."

Ben sat back in his rolling chair and crossed his hands on his chest. "This is going to be an interesting story. What happened?"

"It's about that necklace." I filled him in on Jimmy's visit and the police interview.

Ben set down a well-chewed pencil. "There's something about that necklace that makes that family crazy. What do we know about Celeste Wilson?"

"Just what I told you. Agnes said Celeste left, and she didn't know where she was."

Ben pulled out a phone book and leafed through it. Running his finger down the page, he stopped. "Well, I'll be."

"What?"

"Look at that address. Isn't that where the new strip mall is going in?" He pushed the phone book toward me.

"Oh, yes. She was one of the renters displaced when the plans for the project came about."

"Don't you get it? She was in the way."

"Not from what Jimmy told me."

"And that's interesting as well."

"I know, but I still feel like Harry is suspicious. When he spoke to me about Agnes and Celeste, he definitely sounded jealous of her friendship with his wife."

"Then you need to ask him." Ben looked up at the clock. "I'd love to go with you to talk to Harry, but I have a deadline, and if I don't get on it, I'll be delivering papers, not writing for them."

I wouldn't have minded him going along but nodded. "I can talk to him. You just get to work."

Even though it had been a long day, I was certain Harry would be at the VFW hall with his WWII buddies. Jimmy had told me that's how his dad usually spent his evenings.

When I entered, I heard a wolf whistle in the background. These guys might be old, but they weren't dead. I found Harry sitting at the bar with a couple of other men.

"I need to speak with you."

Harry's eyebrows rose. "Here?"

"If you don't mind. It will only take a minute."

"I suppose." He looked to the other two men. "Excuse me, fellas. Seems I have a date."

They both smiled as if it were perfectly normal for a woman my age to come pull one of them away from their endless war stories.

Once seated, I wasted no time. "How did you feel about Celeste and your wife?"

"What do you mean? How did I feel about Celeste?" His lower lip firmed as Harry filled a pipe from a tobacco pouch. "Couldn't stand the woman." He struck a match and lit the tobacco.

"How did you feel when you found out that Celeste Wilson had gone missing?"

"I hardly see why this is important to you, young lady." His eyebrows fused together for a moment as he inhaled on the pipe. "Hold on a minute. What are you implying?"

"How much time did your wife spend with Celeste?"

"Too much time if you really want to know. They called each other every day. They went to all those infernal clubs together. If you ask me, it was a waste of time. She belonged at home, not out gallivanting the town with that woman."

"Didn't your wife's problems start after Celeste disappeared?"

Harry looked down at the tabletop. "Yeah, after. To me, that was just proof Celeste had been a bad influence on her. She left Agnes a wreck. What kind of friend does that? Not telling her anything. Trust me, Dot, I know. Celeste was no good."

"But your wife told me they were friends since childhood."

"Who cares? I'm the one she married."

I was going down a road that would have no answers, so decided to change the subject. "How tall are you, Harry?"

He scowled. "Six two. Why does it matter?"

"Oh, nothing. You just seem like you're as tall as my dad."

"You know I liked you even though Jimmy kept telling me things about you that were awful. Now I'm thinking maybe Jimmy was right. You are strange."

"Do you remember Celeste wearing a certain necklace?"

"The women exchanged jewelry every year. I don't know. You're asking the wrong guy. Now, if you'll excuse me, I need to get back to my friends."

I had to keep going, so blurted out before he could stand, "Do you know how to run an excavator?"

"Of course, I do." His chin jutted out. "I founded Gibson Construction. Why wouldn't I?"

"When was the last time you were on an excavator?"

Harry stuttered. "I don't know. Years ago." He looked closely at me. "What's this all about?"

"It's really nothing, Mr. Gibson. I'm just trying to straighten out some

146

facts surrounding the three deaths."

"Three deaths? Don't you mean two?"

"I'm including Celeste."

"Celeste went off somewhere. She's not dead. I don't know where you're getting your facts, but you couldn't be more wrong."

I leaned closer. "Maybe, but whose bones are behind Jimmy's rental house?"

Chapter Twenty-Six

The next morning, Mary called before work. "Sorry to call so early, but I knew you wouldn't be able to talk once you started working with the kids."

"That's okay." I glanced at the clock.

"I talked to Arturo last night."

"Did you find out anything?"

"Not much. Yes, he hated Milton, but he didn't have kind words for Elwood, either. Seems they'd locked horns a few times."

"We knew that already. My question is, did he hate them enough to kill them? Then we also have Celeste. There doesn't seem to be any connection between her and Arturo."

"Actually, there was. You forget he runs a service company. When Jimmy was too cheap to make repairs on her rental house, she called on Arturo's company. He didn't know her well, he said, but she was a customer." The kids were making noise in the background. "Sorry, I have to get the kids off to school. I wish you were back in an office. It would be a lot easier to call you that way."

If only I were. I was longing for an office job when I arrived at Clancy's Department Store ten minutes late. My mind was still on my conversation with Mary, and how Arturo seemed to be holding back. Where was he when Milton was killed? If I had to bet on it, he was with Isabella, but because they would probably want custody of Freddie, their being together might make Isabella look like an unfit mother. What would Arturo have to do with the other murders, Celeste Wilson and Elwood Kirk? No, Arturo was a slimy guy, but I doubted he had anything to do with Milton's murder. As I made my way to the back of Clancy's Department Store, Santa was sitting on his throne, reading the *Camden Courier*. Children were starting the backup around the corner, and Mr. Clancy was standing at the front of the line looking perturbed.

"Sorry. Traffic." There was no traffic in Camden, Texas.

Mr. Clancy shook his head. "This is not good. I'm going to cut your hours down to part-time, Dot. Sadly, you've proved unreliable. You show up late, take long lunches, and I suspect you're leaving early. I have asked Mrs. Clancy to fill in during the afternoon. That should give you more than enough time to see to your personal issues."

I did the math. "But you open at nine. That gives me only a few hours a day."

"Well then, maybe you should've thought of that before you adopted a habit of showing up late. Photos with Santa are very profitable for us during the Christmas season. If we continue to have angry parents walking away with their children, what's to stop them from going down to the hardware store where they have Buck Phillips?" Buck Phillips used to shoe horses, but now retired, he worked during the holidays as a Santa. Every time I was around him, I thought he still smelled a little horsey.

A very unhappy elf came toward me, her shoes giving a forced jingle as she plodded along.

"Mrs. Clancy will train with you this morning." Mrs. Clancy gave her husband a sideways glance that was not positive. She was much taller than Dot, and her legs were so thin that the peppermint tights looked like candy canes. She had pinned her elf hat on top of a pile of bouffant hair, and the look on her face was not happy Christmas. It must've taken a lot of convincing to get Mrs. Clancy in that costume.

"Today's hours will not go on your timesheet, Dot." Mr. Clancy said succinctly.

"But I'm here, and I'm working." This was going from bad to stupid.

"Let's just call this a lesson, shall we?"

"That's not fair."

"And I think the police questioning me about your activities is unfair. I have a business to run here, something I don't think you understand. I turned a blind eye to you losing your last job, but maybe I should have trusted my instincts. You have some serious discipline problems, young Missy. Maybe you should find a nice husband instead?"

"Why would I need to do that?"

"Why don't you take the day off? I can instruct Mrs. Clancy."

Sitting in my car a minute later, Mr. Clancy's words echoed in my brain. *Maybe you should find yourself a nice husband.* The undertone was that a man would make sure that I would be on time, or even worse, a woman's place was only in the home. He made a husband sound like a glorified father. Had I been a man, would he have said a *wife* would keep me in order? I leaned my head on the steering wheel, trying to think about how I would have enough money to pay this month's rent. A rude hammering on the window made me jump. Jimmy's face was inches from the glass.

His muffled voice came through the window. "I need to talk to you."

The last person I wanted to talk to was Jimmy Gibson. Given a choice, I felt more like doing bodily harm to my former boss than passing small talk on the street.

"I'm busy," I said.

"Sleeping in your car?"

"What?" I snapped. Hopefully, he would think I couldn't hear him and would give up trying to talk to me.

"Roll down the damn window." Against my better judgment, I cranked the window, lowering the glass.

"What?"

"I'd like to know where you thought you had the right to give that necklace to the police. They've been on my back all morning."

This was where I should have felt sorry for Jimmy, being pressured by the local constabulary. But inside, I felt a sick little beam of happiness. I was happier than I had been all day. Cocking my head slightly, I gave him a smile, my voice taunting. "What's the matter, Mr. Gibson? Is not getting your way bothering you? People who don't work for you don't have to listen to your

150

bull."

"What are you talking about? You blatantly stole that necklace, and when the police found out you had it, you gave it to them. You did this on purpose just to spite me. Try to deny it."

I tried to keep my voice, in direct contrast to his, low and controlled. "I'm not denying anything. I'm glad the police took it away from me. Why do you care so much about it? You know something about Celeste Wilson's disappearance that the rest of us don't know?"

Jimmy clenched his fists at his side. I waited for his answer but was afraid it would be a punch in the face. I leaned away from the window opening.

"This is a small town, Dot. You're going to find that there are some people in Camden you don't cross. I'm one of those people. I'll make sure you never work as a secretary anywhere else. If there is a job advertised in this town, you can bet I'll call them before you can get your application filled out. It's my public duty, don't you think? Messing with me is the biggest mistake you'll ever make."

I decided to ignore Jimmy's threats. He only had power if I gave it to him. "Did the police ask you about more than the necklace?"

"Sure, they did, and you know what I told them? I told him to question you. I'm sure they'll be calling. Maybe they'll let you work in the warden's office at prison. I hear they have a lot of filing there."

"What would be my motive? Why would I kill Milton? Why would I kill Elwood? I didn't even know the woman who rented your house."

"Don't you worry about that. I'll make sure there's some connection the police believe."

"Then you'd be lying."

"Yet who will they believe? I have more credibility in this town than you ever will." Jimmy drew closer to the open window, his face near enough for his nose to touch me. His furious breath was on my face. "Stop what you're doing. Or you'll be sorry." He reached through the window and placed his hand on my shoulder, squeezing it so tightly I gasped. "Do you understand me? Don't mess with me or with my father or my mother. I'll make sure that the police keep you away from my home. My family needs to be protected from disgruntled employees. You're no more than a girl with a typewriter." He unclenched my shoulder and stepped back, putting on a smile. He grinned at passersby as his Texas drawl coated his threat. "You have a real nice day now, and Merry Christmas to you, Dot, darlin'."

I was shaking when I got home. Arlene brought me a cup of tea, and I recounted my conversation with Jimmy. Arlene sat next to her crochet basket with her latest work thrown on top. "You want me to call your mother? How about your father? They should know about this, Dot."

"That's okay. I'll be fine. Just, it was all so cold. I had no idea Jimmy Gibson could be such a mean man."

"Neither did I. The question is, do you think he'll follow through?"

"I don't think I want to find out."

"If you won't let me call your parents, how about that nice young man from the newspaper you seem to spend so much time with? Why don't you call him?"

I wasn't sure how Ben would react to my meeting with Jimmy, but the thought of his arms around me right now was tempting. "Maybe I will."

"Great idea. I'll go in the next room so you can have some privacy if you want to use my phone."

When Arlene left the room, I lifted the black table phone and dialed the newspaper office. "Yes, can you connect me to Ben Dalton's desk?" There was a clicking, and Ben came on the line.

"Ben Dalton."

"Hey, Ben," I said shakily. "You have a minute?"

"What's wrong, Dot? Did you get fired again?"

If he only knew. "Not fired, but Mr. Clancy cut me to part-time."

"Oh, I'm so sorry. I'm probably part of the reason. I think I caused you to come back late one day."

"It wasn't you. He has his wife working afternoons now, so I'm still trying to figure out how I'm going to pay my rent. But there's more."

"Something else is wrong?"

"Jimmy threatened me today."

I heard the wheels of Ben's chair creak. I could tell he was sitting up straighter at his desk. "Threatened you how?"

"He told me to stay away from his family, and he was going to file a harassment charge with the police."

"He can do that?"

"I don't know, but he said if I came near their house, he would call the police and that I wasn't to talk to his mother or his father. He also told me to stop putting my nose into the Milton investigation."

Ben was quiet on the other side. Then he said, "Did he hurt you? Because if he hurt you, he'll be talking to me next, and I may not be talking."

My knight in shining armor. "All he did was squeeze my shoulder. He didn't hurt me."

"Just enough to make you scared, but not enough to leave a bruise. I know the type."

"What am I going to do?"

"I don't know, but I'm on my way over. Are you at home?"

"Yes."

"I'll be right there." As I hung up the phone, I realized something. This was the first time in my life I had been troubled and not gone to my parents. I had called Ben. I almost felt ashamed when I remembered Mr. Clancy's comment. *Go find yourself a husband.* Was I that shallow?

Chapter Twenty-Seven

When Ben arrived, I was upstairs in the apartment. Arlene made no complaint about Ben going upstairs. She even seemed to approve of it. He walked in and immediately took me into his arms. No kiss, but a very warm hug. I couldn't deny how safe I felt. I relaxed and retold the story of my encounter with Jimmy.

"You're just lucky he didn't hit you. I suppose being right there in the middle of downtown and in front of Clancy's Department Store stopped him. Just out of curiosity, what have you dug up the last day?"

"You mean besides the fact that someone probably buried Celeste Wilson behind her own house? I talked to Harry and Arturo, and I still don't know. They have alibis, and neither one of them has a motive for killing all three people. Maybe we're talking about two murderers on the loose?"

"Maybe. But after today, we have to look at Jimmy."

"Jimmy wouldn't kill his own brother."

" You can't deny he has a hot temper, though."

Ellie came slamming through the door carrying a large bag. "My destiny is changing. I got Mildred Farmer to watch the store. She's going to take care of day-to-day business and mail me reports." She clanged the suitcase against her thin legs. "I borrowed this bag from my friend Stacy. It's what she used when she went on her European tour. I think it's big enough to live out of for a while."

Ben surveyed the battered brown bag that if it could talk, held a history of its own. "Are you sure you want to drag that thing around? Once you fill it up, it'll probably weigh a hundred pounds."

Ellie put the bag on the ground and took a breath. "I can stand a little inconvenience because I'm going to a place where people have nothing this nice."

"That's very noble of you, but I'd like to see how you feel about it after carrying it around for a month," Ben suggested.

I blew out a breath. She was really doing this. "When does Mildred take over?"

"Tomorrow." Ellie raised both fists in the air like she was coming across a finish line. "Yes sir, ask not what your country can do for you, but what you can do for your country. I'm taking a bus to New York and then a ship to Africa."

"So soon?" I was scrambling to figure out how I would meet my own portion of the rent this month. Now, with Ellie gone, I'd have to pay double.

Ellie stepped over to the couch. "I know it's soon. In twenty-four hours, I will begin the next part of my life."

"What does Al say about all of this?"

"Who cares? This is bigger than me and Al. This is bigger than Camden, Texas, or the Blue Bonnets dress shop. This is life. I finally feel like I'm living."

It was ironic that it took seeing someone dying for Ellie to figure out she needed to start living. Her approach to this was exciting to her, but to me, it looked a little crazy. "Have you spoken to him?"

"Oh." She pushed away the air with her hand. "I'll send him a postcard from New York. He's a smart guy. He'll figure it out."

Ben's jaw dropped slightly. "Boy, that's tough on a guy. I wouldn't want to be the one in love with you."

Ellie sat in the chair across from us. She leaned forward, her gangly elbows on her knees, her hands on her chin. "I don't know how to explain this to you, but I am out of the realm of the ordinary. I am embarking on a whole new adventure in my life. An adventure where I will help other people, and I will take this crazy world and make it just a little better. Does that make sense to you?"

It made sense to me on one level, but it was crazy. "Why do you have to go so far to do it? If you want to help people in this world, we have a mission in town. We have an orphanage on the edge of town, and those kids always need things. With your sewing skills, you could have clothes for those kids that they would be proud of. There are so many ways to serve others besides getting on a ship and going over to another country."

"Are you saying America is more important than other countries?"

Ben clucked his tongue. "No. Of course not, but the phrase you keep insisting on repeating to us is 'ask what not your country can do for you but what you can do for *your* country.' This is your country, Ellie."

Ellie gave out a gasp of exasperation. "You don't understand. No one seems to understand." Her tone turned angry. Why was she angry when she was the one acting irrationally? "I have to pack. I don't have time for this right now. I just hope I can sleep tonight." She walked back, snatched up the bag, and walked to her bedroom. I put my hands over my face in frustration, then released them in a burst of anger. "Great. How am I going to pay Ellie's rent and mine? I just have to hope she made arrangements with Arlene downstairs."

"If she hasn't talked to Al, then she hasn't talked to Arlene. I wonder if she's talked to her mother?" Ben asked.

"I better call. The way she's moving, I doubt she's told anybody."

"I get that," Ben said. "The fewer people you tell, the fewer people you have to explain yourself to. She just wants to go and never look back."

"I wish we had never gone to Dallas."

"Which reminds me, did you get your film back yet?"

I felt a headache forming behind my temple. "I dropped off the film, but frankly, I forgot to pick it back up again. I'm sure it's at the drugstore."

"How about I take you out for an ice cream sundae, and we look at the pictures?"

"Sure."

"Nothing says healing like ice cream." Ben smiled.

Chapter Twenty-Eight

The photos did little to settle my sense of unrest as I gazed at the somewhat blurry shots of the end of JFK's life. Thankfully, they were too blurry to use in the *Camden Courier*, so Ben didn't ask. I had been so excited to use my new camera that day, but once we finished looking at the developed film, I threw the camera in the trash. I would buy another, different camera. I never wanted to have that camera in my hands again, nor the memories it brought with it. I would also burn the pictures and the negatives before Ellie could see them. Who would save pictures of such a horrendous event, anyway?

At the end of our evening, Ben stood at the front door of Arlene's house, hesitating. He shifted from one foot to the other, stuck his hands in his pockets, and then pulled them out again. Would he ever kiss me?

"Well, good night." His gaze drifted from my eyes to my lips. That had to be a good sign.

"Good night." I took a nervous swallow. "Thank you for everything."

Ben whispered, "Anytime, Dot. Just call."

Finally, after what had seemed like an eternity, Ben leaned forward and lowered his lips onto mine. Arlene's TV played in the background, but as the kiss deepened, the sound faded. Finally, he pulled away.

The smile on his face would star in my dreams that night. "I'll see you tomorrow, but in the meantime, promise me you'll stay out of trouble."

"I promise."

Ben skipped down the front steps. He tilted his fedora back, just slightly, and I couldn't miss the lilt in his long legs.

The phone was ringing in the background, and Arlene's voice pulled me out of my reverie. I hadn't realized she was standing on the porch next to me. "Joe Columbo from the diner is on the phone for you. He wants you to come down."

I turned and followed Arlene into the house. "What for?"

"I'm not sure." She handed me the phone. "You talk to him."

"Dot, I'm so glad I caught you. I have little Freddie Gibson down here. He wants you to come and get him."

"Freddie? Why me? Where's his mother?"

"That's what I asked him. We tried to call his mother, but she didn't answer."

"What about the Gibsons?" I had only spoken to the child twice and found it hard to believe he would ask for me.

"That's a no-go. He says he is afraid of Jimmy. He wants you."

I glanced at my watch. "I'll be at the diner in five minutes."

When I walked in, little Freddie was sitting in a chair next to the cash register eating an Italian pastry. He smiled, revealing two missing teeth on the top.

"Hi, Mith Dot."

"Freddie? What are you doing here?"

Freddie laid down his fork quietly. "I ran away. I'm going to come and live with you," he lisped.

I pulled up a chair next to Freddie. "Me? Why not your mom or your Uncle John?"

"I want to live with you."

I couldn't help but wonder if this had something to do with the elf costume. What kid wouldn't want to live with someone who had the inside track to the North Pole?

Mr. Columbo came up with a dishrag in his hand. "Thank you for coming down here. I saw him sitting outside for a long time, so I asked him to come in. That was when he told me he was running away."

"Can I borrow your phone?"

"Sure." He lifted a heavy black phone from under the counter and put it down.

Freddie's eyes got big. "Who are you calling?"

"Your Aunt Mary."

"But she will call my mother."

"Maybe your Aunt Mary will let you spend the night with your cousins. Let's call her and ask, okay?" I tried to make my tone light to ease the little boy's anxiety. After a brief conversation with Mary, she promised she would get hold of Isabella, and someone would pick him up shortly.

"So, I have a question." Mr. Columbo came over with a pastry for me, but then turned to Freddie. "Why is it you want to run away from home?"

Freddie had to be in a fragile state after losing his father. He resembled Milton in a lot of ways, maybe even including searching me out as a friend.

"Because Papa Arturo doesn't like me."

Now it was making sense. "What do you mean he doesn't like you?" Joe Columbo pulled up a chair. "He seems like a nice man."

Arturo had never been overly nice to me, personally, but I had hoped he was a little less abrupt with Milton's son.

Freddie swung a foot that didn't quite reach the floor. "He says I'm messy and loud. He tells me to go to my room all the time. He doesn't even like baseball."

Arturo had no children of his own, so maybe becoming the father of a rambunctious little boy was more than he could handle. "Have you talked to your mother about this?"

"She won't listen to me. She says I'll get used to him. I don't like him. He's not a nice man. I wish my daddy was here." A single tear fell down his cheek as his bottom lip puffed out.

I put my arm around Freddie. "I wish he was here, too. He'd know just what to do."

A few minutes later, the door to Columbo's opened, and Arturo stepped inside. Freddie's arm tightened around me. He whispered, "Don't let him take me, Mith Dot. Let me stay here with you."

Arturo walked over, each step sounding like a drumbeat to the gallows. "Freddie, what are you doing here? Do you realize how much trouble you're in, young man?"

"I won't go with you!" Freddie screamed. "You can't make me. You're not my daddy. Go away."

Arturo's gaze bounced from Freddie to me. "I should've known you'd be behind this. Your interference is not welcome. Step away from the boy."

I spoke through gritted teeth. "I'll do nothing of the sort, and for your information, Freddie called me because he couldn't get a hold of Isabella. I am not interfering, and I deserve an apology for that."

"Well, you'll be waiting a long time because I don't intend to apologize for anything." He looked over at Mr. Columbo and nodded. "Take care of the kid for a minute. I need to talk to Dot."

"I need to go to the bathroom," Freddie said.

"Come along," Joe said. He turned his gaze to Arturo. I wasn't sure if it was an announcement or a warning. "We'll be just a minute."

Arturo motioned to the alcove where patrons waited for tables. "I don't think I've made myself clear. You need to butt out of my business. There are others who can tell you what happens when you mess with Arturo Galvez." He drew closer, making me nervous. He put a hand on either side of my face. "Do you understand?" Arturo had me backed up against the wall, and if I wanted to escape, it would be difficult.

Another bully. It was so easy to quiet a woman when a man outweighed her. This wasn't happening, especially after what I had gone through with Jimmy. I jerked away from his grasp. "What are you so afraid of?"

"I'm not afraid of you."

"I think you are. The story of your affair with Isabella is out, so I can't do any more harm with that, which leads me to think that there's more to this. Could you be hiding something to do with Milton Gibson's death? Just how well did the police check out your alibi? You told them you were with Isabella, a woman in love with you enough to lie for you. Is that the case?"

There was rage in Arturo's eyes as he pulled one hand back to slap me across the face. Before he could contact my cheekbone, another hand came in and grabbed it, pulling it back. When I looked up, my rescuer was the last person I would have expected.

"Jimmy? What are you doing here?" I asked.

"It looks to me like I'm saving your ass." He turned to Arturo. "It isn't nice to hit a lady. You need to back off." He let go of Arturo's wrist.

"This is between me and Dot. She's butting in over the boy." Arturo grabbed me under the arm and pulled me back to Freddie who was just coming back into the room with Joe.

"Freddie?" Jimmy had just caught sight of the little boy.

"Yes," Arturo said. "Freddie called your secretary here and decided that he wanted to go and live with her. I was explaining to her she needs to mind her own business and not interfere in mine."

Jimmy let out a little laugh and placed a hand on his forehead. "Here you are again, Dot, in trouble because you can't let things alone. Arturo, old man, I know what you're talking about because I speak from experience. Dot is no longer my secretary for that very reason. Can't stop interfering."

I held both hands flat up in the air. "Wait one minute. I'm in the room, and I can hear you both. Not that I want to. Freddie called me, I didn't call him. I have done nothing but be a friend to Freddie, and yet you two sit here like two crowing roosters in the same barnyard. For your information, this little gathering is not about me. It's about Freddie. He's afraid to go home with you, Arturo. He says you're mean to him."

Arturo blew out a sound with his lips. "Freddie doesn't know what he wants."

"Well, he knows what he doesn't want. He doesn't want to be around you. Look at him." I motioned toward Freddie. "He's a little boy who has just lost his father. Have either of you taken that into account?"

"I have," said Jimmy. He walked over to Freddie. "What if you come home with me? You're a Gibson, son, and you should live with the Gibsons."

Freddie's answer was ear-splitting. "NO." He pulled away from Joe and ran over to me, wrapping his arms around my waist. "No. I don't want to go with you. You're mean, too."

"He doesn't like you either," Arturo laughed. "All he wants is little Dot here."

"That's fine. He can go with Dot." Jimmy's words were a surprise to me. He fought like hell to get his necklace back but gave up his nephew with little argument. "But I repeat, Freddie is a Gibson and belongs with the Gibson family. We'll be filing for custody, and you, sir, have no legal right in this matter."

The look in Arturo's eyes was something between anger and panic. "The judge will never grant you custody. They always rule in favor of the mothers. You're just wasting your time and money."

"We'll just see what the judge says." Jimmy was uncharacteristically calm.

The door opened, and Isabella ran in, with Mary right behind her. Isabella came straight for Freddie. "Freddie, Freddie. What are you doing? Why did you run away?" Freddie loosened his grip on me and ran to his mother.

"I don't want to live with Papa Arturo."

Isabella became quiet as her eyes beamed upward at Arturo. "Papa Arturo is good to us. We love Papa Arturo. Come now, let's go home." She took Freddie's hand and walked to the door. Shoulders slumped, he obeyed his mother, but as he walked to the exit, he turned back, his eyes besieging me. I felt sorry for the little guy but had no idea what I could do for him. Arturo turned and followed. Jimmy called after him.

"This isn't over yet."

Arturo ignored him, and Jimmy turned to me. "I wouldn't want to live with that man either," Jimmy said.

"I guess I should thank you. If you hadn't interfered, he would've hit me for sure."

"Yeah, well," Jimmy shuffled his feet slightly, his gaze on his shoes. "We all have our moments."

At the counter, Mr. Columbo pulled up a large white bag of food. "Here's your order, Jimmy."

"Thanks." Jimmy turned back to me. "See you in the funny papers."

Chapter Twenty-Nine

The next morning, after a fitful night of sleep, I prepared to take Ellie to the bus station. "Explain to me one more time why Al is not doing this? Seems to me you would want to have just a little more time with the man."

"Al has a business to run," Ellie said, shuffling off the comment. "We'll stay in touch, don't you worry."

She made it sound so simple. She was leaving the man she had been pining after for almost ten years but acted as casually as she would telling the paperboy to stop delivering for a week. Ellie had traded her common sense for a fantasy she had concocted. She was so busy planning her crusade that she was neglecting her own life, and there was nothing Al or anyone could do to stop it.

"I think you're making a mistake," I said as Ellie walked to the next room to pull her suitcase off her bed. "You're breaking Al's heart. Have you considered that?"

Ellie dragged the enormous bag out of the bedroom. She'd spent her entire night packing it, and it looked to be well over the hundred pounds that Ben predicted. "Al is a big boy. He'll be fine. He understands how important this is to me, and you worry too much."

We barely spoke on the drive to the bus station. Ellie was no doubt dreaming of her adventurous fantasy life while I was trying to think of something I could say to change her mind. After parking, I walked inside while Ellie attempted to drag the suitcase. "You want me to help you carry that?" I asked.

"No, no. I need to get used to it. Give me a couple of days on the road, and it won't bother me at all."

Spoken like a cockeyed optimist.

We stood under the bus schedule, searching for the bus that would take Ellie to Dallas, where she would board another bus that would take her to New York. The second bus would take three days to get to the Big Apple. Just the bus trip to get to the ship was arduous. Ellie didn't even like long road trips to Houston.

"There it is. Oh, that's a surprise. It looks like it boards in about ten minutes." Ellie took a quick breath and bit her bottom lip. "We got here just in time. The bus is running according to schedule."

She rushed to the ticket counter and purchased a ticket. She was jabbering on as we walked to the bus platform when a deep voice came from behind her. "Ellie." Al stood just a few feet away with Ben next to him.

"You didn't have to come down here," Ellie said, sounding more aggravated than happy to see him.

"You know I would want to be here. If Ben hadn't come over and told me you were taking a bus this morning, I would've had no idea. You were sneaking out of town like some sort of thief. So, I don't mean enough to you for you to at least let me say goodbye?"

"It's not a big deal, Al. I'll be back before you know it." Ellie made such light of her trip and seemed to be blind to what the rest of us could clearly see—she was breaking Al's heart. His chin wavered. From the look on his face, Al couldn't figure out why the woman he was planning to marry was getting on a bus to travel to the ends of the earth.

Ellie took off her white gloves and stepped closer to Al, but not close enough for him to touch her. "You mean the world to me. You know that."

"Then why are you leaving me?"

"Because I need to." Her explanation was weak, and the statement she had made earlier about how Al understood what she was going through was clearly a lie she had been telling herself.

"What if *I* need you here? What if I need you to marry me?"

"I thought we settled that. We are no longer engaged. I'll be back before you know it. Please Al, I just have to do this."

"This is crazy, Ellie. You *don't* have to do this. You want to help somebody? Help me. Some days I can't even match my own socks. Help the people who get offerings from the church. Help your neighbor mow his grass, babysit, donate blood, but why the hell do you have to help somebody on another continent? Why do you have to go so far away?" His last statement softened as Al came to the edge of an emotional breakdown.

Ellie looked up at the clock and then back at Al. Her expression was one of confusion. "I thought you loved me. I thought you understood what I was going through after seeing what happened in Dallas. I guess I was wrong. Start dating somebody else, Al. Don't bother waiting for me." She turned and picked up the suitcase, intending to hurry to the waiting bus, but the weight of her parcel slowed her down, leaving her dramatic last words flat. Pulling the suitcase up the stairs of the bus, Ellie quickly found a seat, but instead of looking out the window and waving as other passengers did, she looked forward.

I walked over and slipped my hand under Al's elbow. "I'm sorry. I tried to talk her out of it, but she just wouldn't listen to me."

"She is the stubbornest woman I've ever met." His voice broke. "And I'm going to miss her every minute of every day. I just don't know how she could do this to me, to us."

Ben came to Al's other side and put an arm around his shoulders. "Women," Ben said. I shot Ben a scowl. "Can't live with them and can't live without them."

Al shook his head. "So true, brother. So true."

"Can we buy you a cup of coffee or something?" I said as the bus pulled away.

Al looked out at the departing vehicle as if he wanted to see every bit of his bride-to-be before she disappeared. "That's real nice of you, but I think I need a little time alone."

As Al walked away, I closed the gap between Ben and me. "This is awful."

"Like you said, you tried to stop her. I thought maybe bringing Al here would change her mind."

"I'm glad you brought him to the station. He deserved a last word with Ellie. She was going to cut him right out of this."

"It was easier for her. No emotional goodbyes, no guilt. As a confirmed bachelor, I'm ashamed to admit it's the easiest way to end a relationship. Oh, but I am glad to see you today."

I hit Ben on the shoulder. "Really? Now I know the truth."

"I'd never do that to you."

"Sure. So why is it you're happy to see me today?"

"I did some research into Elwood Kirk's background."

"What did you find out?"

"Elwood had a bit of a gambling problem. He was in debt up to his eyeballs, but the people at the bar said he had a wad of cash the night he got beaten up."

"That right there is motive for murder. If everyone in that bar saw the cash, someone could have lured him into the alley and killed him. Simple as that."

"You're right, and I'm sure that's probably the theory the police will go with. Something else I learned about Elwood. Did you know he was married?"

I kept asking myself what fool would want to marry Elwood Kirk? He wasn't a bad looking man, but he was mean, and that makes anyone ugly. "I had heard he was married but I've never met his wife."

"That part doesn't matter as much as the police were called to his house twice because he was battering her."

"Given the time I spent with Elwood, that's not much of a surprise. He was a terrible bully to Milton and everyone else around them. He was one of those guys that got pure joy out of watching somebody else suffer."

"Funny you should bring up Milton. What if Elwood killed Milton?"

"Milton was the victim of blunt force trauma. Elwood seemed like someone who rather beat him to death with his fists. Just a theory."

"I agree."

"Mary said the wound was circular like a hammer."

"A hammer?"

"Are you trying to tell me that a construction foreman wouldn't have a hammer in his truck? Those guys travel with their own toolboxes."

Ben nodded. "Okay, then Elwood could have done it."

"But why? He liked to pick on Milton, but he didn't have enough motive to kill him."

"Unless you say to yourself," he put his hand up in the air as if he had just gotten a brilliant idea, "just how mean was Elwood?"

Before leaving the bus station, I picked up a copy of that day's *Camden Courier* from the newsstand. If I were going to plan to pay my rent after the first of the year, I had to have another job. I'd start with the classifieds, and then, if I found nothing there, I'd go to the job board at Hudson Secretarial School.

After saying goodbye to Ben, I stopped by the library and spread my newspaper out on one of the large reading tables. I also wanted to tell my mother about Ellie leaving. Ellie had forbidden her own mother to come to the bus station, so my mother volunteered to get in touch with Ellie's mom and let her know her daughter got on the bus okay.

Thirty minutes later, I was busy writing down phone numbers and addresses from the ads when my mother came over and sat down across from me. "I just got off the phone with your aunt Mavis. She's so upset. We just don't know what has gotten into that girl's head."

"You should've seen Al. He was doing all he could just to keep it together."

Mother put her hand on mine. "I guess we'll just have to wait this out. Sometimes the best thing you can do is let somebody go ahead with their plan, no matter how crazy it might seem. Most of the time, I find they come to their senses eventually." She looked down at the newspaper. "Have you found any jobs yet?"

"I can make sodas at the lunch counter. Oh, and there's this other one if I don't mind getting up early in the morning. I can deliver papers."

My mother pursed her bottom lip. "This is such a bad time of year to be looking for a job, but if you find you have some free time on your hands, I could sure use your help with the Christmas story time hour."

The annual story time could be a fiasco, and I wasn't sure I wanted to be a part of it. My mother had asked me several years in a row, but I was conveniently tied up with school. This year I didn't have an excuse. "What exactly did you have in mind?"

Mother put her hands together in a prayer-like pose, hiding the smile that registered as she heard me agree. "It's going to be so much fun this year. We're doing a Christmastime version of *Wee Willie Winkie.*"

I tried to remember how the children's rhyme went. It was something about a man in pajamas going around and knocking on windows. These days he would get arrested as a peeping Tom. "I don't think I've ever heard of the Christmas version of this story."

"That's because we are making it up right here. Isn't that exciting? What we need you to do is help with some voicing of the people that Wee Willie Winkie awakens."

"You mean like a puppet show?"

"Sort of. We're also giving out little gift bags with bookmarks and peppermints in them. We'll need help with that too."

I was having flashbacks to my days in the Camden Ladies Club. More time-wasting jobs than I could count, but at least this was for my mother and the children of Camden. It wouldn't be that bad.

"Do you think I could borrow your phone? I should probably call and check on Freddie. Just talking about kids made me think of him. He was pretty upset last night."

Mother rose. "Of course. Use the phone behind the counter."

I wasn't sure of Isabella's number, but I had the number to the Camden Police Department memorized. After going through the police operator, they connected me to Mary's desk.

"How's Freddie doing?"

"Not good. He keeps asking to sleep over."

"He told me Arturo was mean to him. Do you think it's really that bad?"

"If it is, we'll never know. Isabella swears Arturo's a saint, and John believes everything Isabella says. All I see is that little boy's eyes begging me to spend the night with the kids. He told me he wished I were his mama. Can you believe that?"

"Have you heard anything more about the Gibsons filing for custody?"

"Yes. Arturo was furious, and they've already served Isabella with paperwork. They're set to be in court in January."

"I don't understand why Isabella can't see through him. He doesn't like the child. He's only there because this will give him a link to Gibson Construction. He's not building a family, he's building an empire."

"You are preaching to the choir, sister."

"So, how do we get Isabella to understand she's being used?"

"Sometimes, I work with abused women. The men here feel like it's easier for abuse victims to talk to me, even though I've never been in their situation. Honestly, I think they just don't want to handle a crying woman. One thing that always surprises me is that the victim still loves the person who's slapping them around. When you talk about filing charges, many of these women act like they're married to a man who would never dream of hitting them. They don't want their child to grow up without a father, even if it's a terrible thing for them. This is part of a psychology that I'll never understand."

Mrs. Partridge, my former third-grade teacher, approached the checkout desk with a pile of books. I gave her a little wave and then lowered my voice. "So, what you're saying is we could never talk her into it."

There was a pause on the other end of the line. "But we could show her."

"How do we do that?"

"We set Arturo up. Do you still have that Dictaphone?"

"Not personally, but I used one at Gibson Construction. I might be able to borrow it." I thought of Jimmy's new secretary. She would let me use it, I was sure.

"Great. Bring it to the park. I'm going to invite Freddie to play with my kids. Isabella gets her hair done today, so I'll schedule it then so that Arturo has to pick him up."

"I like the way you think."

Chapter Thirty

When Mary offered to take Freddie to the playground that afternoon, Isabella and Arturo seemed glad to accept. "That's so nice of you, Mary. Hopefully, this will help his mood. He's been so down since Milton died."

"That's what family is for," Mary told her. What Isabella didn't know was that I would be bringing Jimmy's Dictaphone to get Arturo on tape. Isabella had no idea how her boyfriend treated her son, and Mary figured that if she could hear some of the rude things he said to him, she might change her mind.

"Are you sure this is going to work?" I asked, feeling a little underqualified to be playing Nancy Drew.

"No, but we have to do something." We watched the children for a while, and then Mary left to call Arturo, leaving me alone. The children ran to the swings and then pushed each other around on the merry-go-round, which was a playful version of a giant Lazy Susan with handles on the top. Children could not resist the bright primary colors and the chance to spin around faster and faster. After that, they ran to the teeter-totter, where a boy nearly knocked Freddie off when he jumped down quickly. Some of these playground amusements were almost dangerous, but they were the ones I had grown up with, so they had to be safe.

Mary approached the playground.

"Did you call him?" I asked.

"I sure did. I told him Freddie wanted to go home. He's not too happy, but he's on his way," Mary said.

I went over to the park bench and pulled the Dictaphone out of my bag.

"You go over there behind that bush, and I'll try to guide the conversation in that direction. I don't think he's going to see you, especially if I get him to turn his back," Mary directed.

"Don't get too far turned around, or I won't be able to pick it up on the tape. We have a lot of playground noise in the background that could distort the sound." I stationed myself in the bushes with my Edison Envoy battery-powered Dictaphone. I double-checked that the tiny reel-to-reel tape was rewound and quietly whispered into the microphone. "Testing." I played it back with the sound low. As my own voice came back to me, I knew I was ready. I hoped I could pick up Arturo's voice clear enough to convince Isabella this man didn't care for her son and was simply with her to further his connection to the Gibson money. Just a few minutes later, Arturo pulled up in his car and strode toward the playground.

His voice was gruff, and he hooked an arm through the air as he spoke. "Freddie. We're going."

Freddie was having the time of his life and turned around to face him. "Already? Can I stay just a little longer?"

Arturo was too far away, and Mary attempted to guide him closer to the bushes where I hid. "Arturo, can I talk to you?"

He turned to Mary and scowled. "I'm in a hurry."

"Oh, this will just take a minute. It's important to Isabella that we get to know each other because we'll be related soon, right?" Mary successfully positioned Arturo near the recording device in the bush.

I held the small gray microphone in my hand and extended it as far as the cord would reach. "Freddie," Arturo yelled. "Get your ass over here. We're leaving."

Freddie came over and begged for more time. "Why do I have to go already? I never get to have any fun anymore."

Arturo reached down and grabbed the little boy by the collar of his coat. "You shut your mouth. I don't want to hear anything else out of you. Get in the car." As Freddie struggled against Arturo's grasp, I felt guilty setting Freddie up this way. Somehow, we hadn't considered how rough Arturo might be on Freddie. Arturo turned to Mary. "What do you want to say to me?"

"You're right. You're busy. It can wait." Arturo turned in a huff, making me feel even worse for what Freddie was about to get from his prospective stepfather.

As they drove away, Mary cut through the bushes to me. "Did you get it?"

"I don't know. Let's see." I rewound the tape. When I pushed the start button, Arturo's voice came through loud and clear. "You shut your mouth. I don't want to hear anything else out of you. Get in the car."

As they drove off, I saw little Freddie's eyes staring back at us. This little ruse had worked, but at what cost? Mary squealed. "That's perfect. We did it. All we have to do is play this for Isabella."

When we visited Isabella that evening, she was at home making dinner. Freddie was in the living room coloring in front of the television, and Arturo was reading the newspaper at the table. He looked up when we entered.

"You again?"

"We wanted to speak to Isabella," Mary said. Isabella turned to them, wearing a red apron over black pants and top, looking very Audrey Hepburn.

"We want you to hear something." I placed the Dictaphone on the table and pushed play. There was no doubt whose voice was on that tape and what he was saying. Isabella's eyes grew wide, and her gaze went from the recording device to Arturo.

She walked out to the living room, tearing off her apron. "You talk to my son that way?" Her eyes were now blazing, and he quickly put the paper down and stood, turning on Mary and me.

"What is this? Were you spying on me? How dare you."

"I don't think that's the issue here," I said. "Why don't you answer Isabella? We'd all like to know why you talked to Freddie that way."

"It's not me."

Isabella walked over to the Dictaphone and played it again. After listening to Arturo's words, she turned on him. "It is you."

Freddie raced to his mother's side. "Yes, it is. You said that."

Arturo's ears turned a bright red as the anger spread to his face. "They made all this up. They don't like me and are out to get me."

"You know who else doesn't like you right now? Me," Isabella said. "I hate you so much that I feel like telling Mary and Dot that I wasn't with you the night Milton was killed. What do you think of that?"

Isabella had just crushed his alibi. There was a silence. Switching gears suddenly, Arturo put on a smile that would melt butter. It was scary to watch. He put his arm around the slight Isabella. "Now, my love. Don't go lying just because you're angry with me. Of course, we were together."

"No, we weren't." Isabella took Arturo's arm from around her and stood back. "I only told them what you told me to say, but now I have to wonder. Where were you that night? I was never in love with Milton, but I certainly didn't want him dead. Where were you, Arturo?"

Arturo's upper lip was sweating. Mary would not let the pressure off. "Where were you, Arturo?"

I repeated Mary's words. "Where were you, Arturo?"

Arturo put both hands in the air in frustration. "I was with another woman. We were at the Coach House Motel. You can check the register. I was with Lupe Menendez. And you should talk. You put tranquilizers in his thermos so the two of us could run off for some romantic weekend. Bet they'd love to know about that."

Isabella threw herself at Arturo, scratching his face and screaming at him. I pulled Freddie by the arm and tried to lead him to the living room. He'd been through enough already. Mary tried to settle Isabella down. As I turned up the TV and told Freddie how much I loved the show, in the back of my mind, I was thinking. If Arturo really had been with another woman, he did actually have an alibi. One that would prove he did not kill Milton Gibson.

When I returned home, Arlene was waiting in the front room for me. "The most curious thing happened today. I received a letter from Agnes Gibson."

"And why is that curious?" I asked.

"Because the letter inside is addressed to you. Why would she do such a thing?" Arlene handed over a folded piece of paper that contained spidery scratch marks.

"Did you read it?"

"I read the first three lines before I realized it wasn't for me. She's prattling on about how she and her friend Celeste used to play where the Gibsons are trying to put in a strip mall now," Arlene admitted.

Arlene's confession was genuine, but it might not have been the first time she snooped where she shouldn't have. "Thank you for telling me."

"Why would she send a letter this way? Why not just address it to you?"

"If I had to guess? I would say she doesn't want people in her house knowing she wanted to contact me. I'm not exactly popular with the Gibson men."

I unfolded the letter and read Agnes's words. After finishing, I put it in my pocket and mounted the stairs. "What did it say?" Arlene asked. "Is she all right? I really did just read the first three lines."

"She's fine. Thanks again." This wasn't the right time to share what Agnes had written. I needed to go upstairs and think. I wanted to share this information with someone but wasn't sure who. Mary had been helpful, and her ties to the police department were invaluable, but right now, Isabella's problems were overwhelming her. With what was going on with Freddie, I wasn't even sure she could get away. Mary would want to be involved, but I worried she was being stretched in too many directions.

I called Ben and invited him to Columbo's for dinner. After the kiss we shared, I wondered if he thought I was asking him out on a date. My mother always told me that nice girls didn't ask men out on dates, but that was starting to feel wrong. I was a nice girl, so why was it bad?

As we sat over two plates of Joe Columbo's finest spaghetti, Ben looked up as he twirled pasta on his fork. "Well, we've talked about the weather and who is most ready for Christmas, but you still haven't told me why you called me here."

"Maybe I just wanted to see you." I was stalling, not sure how to approach this.

"Dot, I think I know you by now. You have something on your mind, and from your expression, I would say it was something pretty big."

"You're extremely perceptive, you know that?"

"I'm a reporter," he said with finality. "It comes with the territory. Now spill. What's going on?"

"If I were to have information that might lead to a killer, but I'm not totally sure, and if I'm wrong, could give a killer a chance to get away, what should I do?"

"This is confusing. You know something?" Ben asked.

"Maybe."

"Then, even though I'm dying to write your story, if you are in danger, you should tell the police."

"I don't know if I will. Whenever I talk to the police, they just shoo me away. It's as if they don't think I can think for myself."

"That's because you have the brain of Agatha Christie and the face and body of Sandra Dee. They think you're Gidget, not Miss Marple."

"I just need to confirm this. I need to be really sure before I go to the police."

Ben set his fork down and leaned on his elbow. "I don't think I like the sound of this."

"I don't think it's anything dangerous."

"And I suppose you want me to be along for your plan. I love to write about crime. I dislike being the victim of crime."

"That's fine. I'll do it myself."

"And that's not the best idea, either. Tell me what you know."

If I told him about Agnes's letter, he wouldn't stop until I told the police. She had been afraid of her own husband and what he might have done. He didn't want her having anyone in her life outside her family. If I told the police, then the chance of this falling apart was not just possible, but probable.

"Oh, don't worry about it. I'm just being silly. I wouldn't dream of doing anything dangerous. Now, did you know I'm a speaker at the Camden library story time?"

"I did not. Are you reading a book?"

"You'll just have to see."

"If it involves another elf costume, I'm there." He smiled with a twinkle in his eye.

On Friday, after a few crazy rehearsals, the cast of *Wee Willie Winkie* was ready. The library was packed, mostly because the kids were off for holiday break. My mother had recruited several people for Wee Willie Winkie to visit, including Joe Columbo and Mr. Draper from the drugstore. With just a short rehearsal, I piped up from behind a bookshelf and said my line, "Oh Wee Willie Winkie, for all the children are in their beds, so go back home."

They got Buck from the hardware store to play Santa, and he brought along his son with Down syndrome, Herbert, who starred as Wee Willie Winkie. Most people like him lived in institutions, but Buck would have none of that. Herbert was with him all the time when he wasn't working. During those times, he stayed at home with his mother. The children's focus was on Santa when Harry Gibson stormed into the library. He zeroed in on me and walked over.

"I need to talk to you."

"What about?"

"I think you know what this is about." He pulled me over to a section of the library away from the children. "You need to leave my Agnes alone. She does not consort with townspeople."

When had I consorted with Agnes? I'd only visited her one time, but Harry acted like I was over there every day. "I don't know what you're talking about."

"You don't, do you? The secret letter?"

"What?" I still had Agnes's letter in my pocket, but why would Harry be so upset? The whole reason she had addressed it to Arlene was possibly to avoid this scenario. Harry Gibson had a problem with control. Whether it was his wife or his sons, he was so possessive he didn't want them to even have friends. What had he thought of Isabella? How far would he go to get custody of Freddie?

"I just finished talking to Arlene," Harry said. "She told me how she addressed the letter to her, but inside was a note for you. What was in that note?"

Darn that Arlene. Just a little bit of pressure and she leaked like the side of the Titanic. "I don't think that's any of your business. After all, the note was addressed to me. Not Arlene, and not you."

He snapped his fingers. "Aha. You don't deny that you and my wife have been secretly communicating."

"Can you hear yourself? Why does it matter? Is your wife not allowed to have any friends? Is that what happened to Celeste?"

"What are you saying? If you are implying that I might've had something to do with Celeste's disappearance, you're wrong. I hated that woman, but I didn't make her disappear. She just wandered off to greener pastures, that's all. She was no good."

"I'm finished talking to you." I moved back toward the gathering.

"Mark my words," Harry shouted after me. "You'll be sorry for interfering. Gibson family business is just that. Our business. Butt out."

Herbert, now finished with his candy cane duty, walked up to me. "Was he angry with you? He sure looked angry."

"Sometimes people get that way, Herbert. Mr. Gibson there can't stand it if his wife writes a letter. There's something wrong with that guy."

Herbert's light blue eyes looked me over. "Like a letter to Santa? Something wrong with that guy." He repeated. "Are you okay?"

I looked up, and Ben was strolling into the children's section. "I'm fine. Thanks, Herbert." Ben caught sight of me and raised his hand to wave. Before I could get to him, Herbert put his hands around my shoulders and gave me a hug. "I really think you're great, Dot. Pretty."

"And you were a fantastic Wee Willie Winkie." I glanced over at Ben, who seemed amused at my conversation with Herbert.

"I know. It's the biggest part of storytime." He puffed out his chest. I gave him a hug back and walked over to Ben.

"New friend?"

"Old friend."

"How was story time? I'm afraid I missed it."

"That's okay. It was fine."

"I have about half an hour. I was wondering if you wanted to go get a cup of coffee or maybe a Coke?"

I looked up at the clock on the wall. "I can't."

"Why not?"

"I have an appointment. Can I get a rain check?"

"Sure." After grabbing my bag, I walked out the door, feeling Ben's eyes following me.

Chapter Thirty-One

Because it was after hours, I used the office key Jimmy had neglected to ask me to return and unlocked Gibson Construction. Rather than have to explain to Jimmy why I borrowed the Dictaphone, I would just place it on the new secretary's desk, and no one would ever know. I would also replace the key. As I stepped into the grubby little office, I found Jimmy sitting behind his desk.

"I was wondering when you were going to show up with that thing. You know, I could've reported you for stealing it."

Jimmy never seemed to notice what was going on in his own office, so this was a surprise for me. I gently placed the Dictaphone on Jimmy's desk. "I know. And thank you for not calling the police. I needed it to help a friend." I backed up and stood by the new secretary's vacant desk.

Jimmy picked up the little gray machine and turned it around in his hands. "Doesn't look like you broke anything. And good of you to return it. But that doesn't mean I'm not angry about this. This is Gibson Construction property, and our new girl seems to be frustrated trying to do shorthand. It's tough enough around here with this doohicky, even worse without it. I can't believe I'm saying this, but you were a decent secretary."

"I'm glad you finally figured that out. You need to give the new girl a break. You talk too fast."

"It's the fast talkers in this world that get things done. That's what I'm all about. That's why I'm the Gibson running this business. My father chose me because I'm an achiever."

"Speaking of your father, he just visited me at the library. Seems he doesn't

179

IF I HAD A HAMMER

want your mother to have any friends. Has he always been like that?"

"My father set standards that our family lives by. Milton had trouble with his expectations. There's a reason we're the number one construction company in Camden, Missy. We let nothing get in our way. We also do not bode interference from other people."

"Does that include your mother's friend Celeste?"

Jimmy got up from behind the desk, still holding the Dictaphone, and walked over to the secretary's desk, placing it on the corner. "What is that supposed to mean?"

"Your mother told me the most interesting thing about Celeste. She was hurt when she left because Celeste had told her she'd never leave. Did you force her out?"

"Leases were made to be broken. I was offering her a nice settlement to move on. She took it. That's all there is to it. That she left and never communicated with my mother after that shows you what kind of person she was."

A thought hatched in the back of my mind. I knew I was taking a chance and could feel my whole body shaking. What I was about to do could turn out badly if not done right. I had never been a good liar. Leaning on the desk, I moved my face closer to Jimmy. He didn't move a step. I placed my hand on the desk and clicked on the Dictaphone.

"Your mother says it doesn't make sense."

I waited for Jimmy to say something about the Dictaphone, but instead, he laughed. He hadn't noticed. "What does she know? She's drugged out of her head most of the time anymore. My mother hasn't had a well-formed opinion since 1955."

I had to keep him talking on the chance he would let something slip. "Your mother seems quite lucid to me. So much so that she wrote me a letter about what she thinks happened to her friend."

Jimmy's head turned quickly to me. "A letter? I don't believe you. Let me see it."

"I don't think that's a good idea. Let's just say that she believes Celeste came to a bad end. She also points to you as the killer. She thinks you killed

Celeste and buried her in the woods behind her house. That's why I found the bone back there. It was a piece of Celeste's hand. Your mother is very frightened of you."

Jimmy, his eyes bright and his smile frozen, stared at me. There was a coldness there I had never noticed before, and it put a new type of fear into me. "That's ridiculous, sweetie." His whole tone of voice was changing. It was smooth, almost seductive. Jimmy drew closer. "You don't believe her, do you? You know me, Dot. I wouldn't hurt a fly."

"That necklace was hers, wasn't it?"

"Why do you say that? Generations of families probably lived in that little house. Could have been anyone's necklace."

"Because you and I both know your mother recognized it." Jimmy continued to draw closer, and I stepped back.

"So, what if it was hers? She lived in that house. Maybe one day she was out gardening, and it fell off her neck."

"Is that what you plan to tell the judge?"

"I don't know what you're talking about." He gave me an innocent smile.

"Maybe not, but Milton knew whose necklace that was. Milton, the brother who, to you, was a hopeless clod, but was actually quite smart. He figured it out, didn't he?"

"Milton couldn't figure out how to tie his own shoe. Please." The real Jimmy was coming back.

"That was you out there at the diner arguing with him, wasn't it?"

"No. You sure think you've cracked the case, haven't you?"

"It took me a while, and I'm still not sure about Elwood. How did he play into all of this?"

Jimmy let out a little snort of a laugh. "I underestimated you, Dot. You're smart for a woman with blonde hair and big blue eyes. You'll go far, or maybe you would have gone far." He snickered again. "That son of a bitch was blackmailing me. He thought he could make some money off what he knew. When I got onto him for being a spy for Sawyer Home Builders, he told me he knew about what happened to my mother's friend, Celeste. Like I said before, nobody gets into the Gibson family's way. Killing him was not only easy, but it was also enjoyable. I think it'll be the same for you." Jimmy now quickened his pace and drew closer to me, throwing me up against the wall. His hands were on my throat. I tried desperately to pull his stubby fingers from around my neck, but he was too strong. I had to think of something before I couldn't think at all. Ellie's words from the day we saw John F. Kennedy shot came back to me. *Knee them in the crotch, and they sing a new song.* When Jimmy stepped back just slightly to get a better grip on me, I lifted my knee and landed a hard one. With a grunt, Jimmy released me and held onto the injured party. I took that minute to run out of Gibson Construction. My heels clicked down the steps as I ran back to my car. I scrambled for my keys, but my hands were shaking too much to open the door. Jimmy stepped out of the office, limping down the stairs. I took off running. After several blocks, I looked back to see where he was. He was pounding down the sidewalk, still coming for me. Finally, I found myself at the construction site. I dashed to the trees behind the construction equipment. I was in the same place where they found Celeste's body. My ribs were pounding against my heart, and I could barely get my breath. I placed my hands on my knees, sucking in air. Was this the way Celeste had felt?

Jimmy stopped running and walked across the construction site toward me. The lot was empty, and there was no one around who would hear my cries. "You know, killing you will be easy. I'll tell your parents that you got the same cockamamie idea and followed your nutty cousin into the Peace Corps. I tried to convince you it was a bad idea, but you caught the next bus. You young girls with all these crazy notions. Oh, and by the way, there's going to be a new parking lot out here in the next two days. They'll never know you're under it.

I couldn't stay here. I ran to the trees at the back of the lot, the same beautiful trees I noticed the day the houses started coming down. The woods back here were thick. This was where Agnes told me she and Celeste had played as children. I might hide in the woods all night until Jimmy gave up. Then I would come back out if I could find my way back. I ran past a stream and an old bridge. The moon shone down through the trees and lit a path in front of me I hadn't seen before. I put my hand on a tree for balance, and something caught my eye in the moonlight. I could roughly make out a carving in the tree trunk. *A and C friends forever.* This was Agnes and Celeste's tree. Leaves rustled in front of me. Unless Jimmy had outrun me, I trusted myself to be led by the sound. It was as if Celeste was guiding me into the woods, into a safe place. I passed the area that held what was known locally as the "Kissing Bridge." Not long after, I found the rock that Agnes had told me about and covered myself up with brush. Moments later, Jimmy came running past, looking for me. He stepped right in front of me, and I was sure this would be my end, but he stepped away. I stayed in my hiding spot for what felt like forever, and Jimmy made two more passes, still not discovering me. As the minutes ticked by, I decided I needed to take a risk. I had to get out of the woods and to safety. But where could I go?

If I went to my apartment, I could put Arlene in danger. The same for my parents' house, although the idea of running home was very tempting. Even though Ben and I were dating, I didn't know where he lived, and the police station was over five miles away. I waited another few moments as I tried to figure out what my next move would be. As a stillness set in, I quietly made my way to the edge of the trees and came out on Willow Street, a block and a half away from Ellie's dress shop. If I could make my way there, I could break in and use Ellie's phone. The streetlights glared down on the sidewalk, the businesses and stores closed for the night. I stepped close to the buildings, trying to blend in, but when I got to the stoplight at the corner, I would have to make a run for it.

I had made it past one store when I heard a truck motor. I couldn't be sure it was Jimmy, but it sounded like his truck. I dashed into a doorway, hoping he couldn't see my form in the shadows. Sure enough, when the truck went by, I could see Jimmy's hand on the side of the door, his head stuck out as he glanced up and down the street, but at the moment he crossed in front of my hiding place, he was looking on the other side. Luck was with me. He continued to drive down the street, and when I felt he was far enough away, I ran to the next storefront and then the next. Now to cross the street. Two more storefronts to go, and I would be at Blue Bonnets. I stepped in front of the first store and was almost to the second one when the truck motor sounded behind me. He was circling the block. If I could just outrun the truck, I would be in Blue Bonnets using the phone. I darted to the front door of Ellie's store and realized I hadn't thought out how to break the glass. I should have picked up a rock when I was in the woods. I frantically looked around me and then realized there was a loose piece of the curb on the street. Jimmy's truck drew closer and was turning into a parking spot. He had seen me. This was it. I had to hurry. I ran out to the street, grabbed the concrete, and with all my strength, pelted it through the glass. The sound of the glass broke the silence of the night. The motor of the truck turned off. The broken glass scraped my arm as I turned the doorknob. The sound of Ellie's cheery bells rang bizarrely in the background as I fought for my life. The silver tree glowed in the window as the color wheel changed the hue of the branches. I ran to the phone and quickly dialed the police. The desk sergeant answered, and I yelled into the phone in one long string of words.

"I'm Dot Morgan. I'm at Blue Bonnets Dress shop. Jimmy Gibson is trying to kill me."

Jimmy came through the door, glass crunching under his boots. I ran to the back room, locking the door behind me.

Jimmy spoke into the phone. "Hello, Officer. Please excuse this call. We were just joking around. I dared her, and spunky little Dot took me up on it. There's really no emergency here. You have an enjoyable evening, and thank you for all the things you do for our community." He slammed the phone down. "Nice try, Dot, but he's not on his way. You're surprisingly good at getting away from me, but it's over now. Open the door. I'll be quick about it."

The doorknob rattled as Jimmy tried to open it. "You're much smarter than most of the girls they sent me from the secretarial school. Did you know you were my sixth candidate? Most of them were as dumb as a bag of rocks, but not you. But you know what they say, a little knowledge can get you into a lot of trouble. And you, my dear, are in a lot of trouble." The doorknob continued to rattle, and I had to assume that Jimmy was opening it. There were no windows in this room. No doors led to other rooms. If

CHAPTER THIRTY-ONE

Jimmy got in, I would have no escape.

This was the room where Ellie created the beautiful dresses that the women in North Texas wore at their weddings and their fancy parties. I felt my way to the sewing machine. Ellie always kept her sewing scissors next to it. My hand rested on top of them. Usually, Ellie would have a fit if I used her scissors for anything but cutting material, but I was sure that, in this case, I'd have her blessing.

Jimmy kept talking on the other side. "You figured out I killed Milton, and you figured out I killed Elwood, but there was one thing you didn't figure out. I wasn't alone when I killed Celeste. I wasn't the only one who wanted her out of the picture. Celeste refused to move out of that house just because she and my mother played in that area. She was so sentimental it made me sick. She tried to tell me about their history and how that land was so important to them. She'd never been able to afford to buy a house there, so she rented it from me. That stupid old woman thought because I was my mother's son, that I would understand. Fat chance. My father didn't like Celeste either. He's very possessive of my mother, and I have always wanted to make him happy. I was the number one son, and what better thing to do for my father than to tell him I would get that old nagging friend out of his way? We went together and killed her. That's how I got her buried, with my dad's help. Of course, no one will ever know it. My dad will live out his life with my mother's full attention. Everything is perfect now." The door suddenly opened, and Jimmy stood there, hammer in hand. "And now I'll take care of you."

I picked up the scissors and held them in front of me as Jimmy's gaze darted to them.

"Don't come near me, or I'll stab you. I swear I'll stab you."

Jimmy gave me a smile as if I were a small child asking for cotton candy. "You wouldn't stab me. You don't know what you're doing. You've never killed anybody. I killed three people, so, to be fair, I do have the advantage."

I stuck out my chin. "Try it."

"You need to get it through your thick head. I'm the killer here, and you're the victim. There are some things in life that you just can't rise above, and this is one of them."

I felt a hopelessness invade me, the same one I had after I saw Kennedy shot. There are things in life you just can't get away from. Some corners will always hold assassins waiting in buildings. But did that have to be true? Did I have to be the victim in this scene? No. No, I didn't. I had a weapon the same as Jimmy. Sure, he was bigger than I was, but with the right move, he could go down. If he hit me with a hammer, it could take several times to take me down. I promised myself I would not be Jimmy Gibson's fourth victim.

He stepped forward, raising the hammer above him, and I held my breath, closed my eyes, and simultaneously brought the scissors down towards Jimmy's chest. Before I could make an impact, a loud noise came out of nowhere, deafening me. Suddenly, Jimmy's weight was on top of me. Had I stabbed him? Why was it so loud? Scissors aren't loud. Was I hurt? Had he shot me?

"Dot?"

I looked up through the darkness.

"Oh God, please tell me I didn't shoot you. It's so dark in here I couldn't see. Dot?"

I made out the outline of Mary standing there, her hands shaking, holding a gun.

Pushing Jimmy's body from me, I placed my hand on the front of my shirt. No holes. "I'm okay."

I looked down at Jimmy. "But he's not."

Chapter Thirty-Two

December 24, 1963

B en and I crunched through the newly fallen snow as the remaining employees of Gibson Construction cleared the demolition site. It had been a busy day with our families, but we decided to take a quiet winter walk to celebrate Christmas Eve.

"It's hard to believe how much has happened since that first day they tore down these old houses. The thing I couldn't get over was how beautiful the trees were behind the properties. Funny how progress can blot out some of the best things in nature."

Ben squeezed my hand. "Yes, but now that Agnes is taking over Gibson Construction, her only stipulation before she sells it to Arturo Galvez was to clear this plot and make it into a park."

We walked to the edge of the property and then came upon the very trees that sheltered me from a killer. "Once she was off the sedatives Harry was giving her, and she told me about her dream for this lot, I thought it was a wonderful idea. She and Celeste roamed this area as children, and it was the best part of their lives. It's only fitting that now she turns it into a park where generations of children can make their own wonderful memories."

"It surprised me at how quickly she came around once the drugs wore off."

"Yes, and she didn't seem all that upset when they came and arrested Harry for the death of her friend. With the sale of the business, she'll have enough to be comfortable for the rest of her life."

"Yes, but what kind of life would it be when her husband killed the only friend she ever had?"

We now came to the edge of the woods, where the snow lightly frosted the brown and red leaves. Ben looked up at the trees. "I can't believe that this was where you ran in the dark when Jimmy was chasing you. You must've been terrified."

"I was, but it was really strange. The moon was out, and it lit a path for me. Even though I had never walked through this part of the woods before, it was as if I knew exactly where I needed to go. I needed to find Celeste and Agnes's clubhouse. Once I got inside, Jimmy didn't know where I was."

"You're the bravest woman I know."

"I wasn't feeling very brave that night. I know this is going to sound strange, but I felt as if Celeste was guiding me. Even though I couldn't see her in bodily form, it just became easy after what had been so difficult."

"What I am amazed at is that when you are in the office, you thought to turn on the Dictaphone. The police were so happy when they found they had a taped confession from their prime suspect."

"Especially because he ended up dead, and there was no way they could verify my story."

Ben turned and stopped. He took my face in his. "Brilliant, simply brilliant." He kissed me with all the excitement of new love. A chilly breeze blew between us, but I couldn't feel it. Ben's arms were warm and made me feel safe.

As we pulled away, I said, "Well, thank you, Mr. Dalton. That's very kind of you."

"My pleasure." He kissed me again. We held each other for a moment, the still December air around us and the picture-perfect snow around our feet.

"I'm beginning to see the magic of these woods," Ben said.

"Yes. We're so lucky." We walked a little farther, getting closer into the woods to the area called the Kissing Bridge, where a lone figure stood. I remembered passing it the night I ran from Jimmy. Al was leaning both elbows over the side of the bridge, looking out at the water.

"There's a sad sack if I ever saw one," Ben said.

"Yes. He comes out here a lot. Ellie said this was the first place they ever kissed."

"I still can't believe she left the way she did."

"I can't believe she lasted through that bus trip, but she must have. . It looks like Al is ready for a long, hard winter."

There was a cracking in the leaves behind them. We stood quietly as we watched another figure approach Al on the bridge.

Al stood up, lifting his elbows off the railing. "Ellie?"

It *was* Ellie. She walked onto the bridge and stood next to Al. They were almost too far to hear, but my cousin's words rang out across the distance.

"I couldn't go. I tried to. I couldn't go."

Al took Ellie into his arms and kissed her like a thirsty man finding water after a trek through the desert. "Don't ever leave again. Please, we can get married this week or in ten years. I don't care, but don't ever go away from me again, do you hear me?"

"I don't need to, now. When I was standing there in New York City, people crowding in all around me, I felt so all alone. I realized the person I was missing most was you. The person who I didn't even bother to say goodbye to. Can you ever forgive me?"

"You're already forgiven." He kissed her again.

Chapter Thirty-Three

New Year's Eve, 1963

B en twirled me around the dance floor until I found myself next to Ellie, now dancing away to "Louie, Louie" by The Kingsmen. People all around us were blowing on New Year's Eve horns and wearing silly little hats. Ellie and Al were a little different in their dance moves, choosing a soft rhythmic step in line with the music. There was love in Ellie's eyes again as she looked up at her fiancé. The wedding was back on for June, and something in their world had reset. Al dipped his head down and tenderly kissed Ellie on the lips.

"Cut that out, you two. This is a family dance," Ben joked.

Al laughed. "Not my problem tonight. I've got my Ellie back, and it's a new year."

I glanced at the clock on the wall of the school gymnasium. "Not yet. It is still 1963."

"And I don't mind seeing it go out," Ellie said as she and Al stepped back and then moved close together again in an improvised jitterbug. "Nineteen sixty-three was not our best year."

Camelot was over. Jackie was a widow, and John-John would never have his father to salute again.

"But 1964 shows nothing but promise," Ben said, his own eyes shining with love toward me.

Something in me had changed. I was no longer that little girl thinking I

190

would break out in song and dance as I romanticized the world of business. Now I knew how hard my job had been and also how unfulfilling. I needed more, and I knew it. "I don't know about that. I'm unemployed again. I don't know where I'm going to find another job after what happened at Gibson Construction."

Ben held me tighter. "Don't worry. Something will come along. If I know Dot Morgan, if something doesn't happen, you'll make it happen. You're just that kind of person. Hey, I heard the DJ on the bandstand say they need someone at the radio station. That could be a fun job. "

"What would I do at a radio station? I'm not a DJ."

"No, you are not, but you can answer a phone. He said he needed someone to answer the request line while also working as a front office receptionist. You'd get to spend the day listening to the radio. I guess he just bought the place, and if they ever branch into TV, I could be an anchor man," Ben said.

"You mean like a real television station?" I asked.

Ben fingered his lapel. "Yes, and don't you think I'd look good on camera?"

"So maybe this is an opportunity for both of us?"

"Maybe." He smiled, a dimple threatening to take away my sensibilities.

"I don't know about you, but my dogs are tired," Ellie said as she danced next to us. "Al wants to get us something to drink. I need to sit down."

"Me too."

Ben bowed. "Lead the way, ladies. I'll help Al with the drinks."

Ellie and I found a seat on the edge of the dance floor. "I can't believe I'm sitting here," Ellie said as she kicked off her shoes and held her feet up to air them.

"I'm just happy you're here. I'm so glad you came back. Not only was I worried about paying the rent, but I was also worried about you."

"I know. I was out of my head for a while there, but I'm back. And that suitcase. It felt like I had packed a bag full of bricks. My arm still hurts. I think I might have a torn rotator cuff."

"Oh, Ellie," I laughed. "This is where you belong, and Al is who you belong with. I don't think we're the same women who stood on that grassy knoll on November twenty-second. Our life felt like a Technicolor musical, but in that horrible second, it turned into a black-and-white movie."

"Oh my, you're eloquent tonight. Ever thought about being a writer?"

"Come on. You know what I'm trying to say."

"Indeed, I do. It took me going 1500 miles dragging something the weight of all my grief to realize that. There is no place like home. There are no people like the people in Camden, Texas."

"Amen to that," Al said as he took the seat next to Ellie, then handed me my drink.

He glanced up at the clock.

"Drink up, ladies, because the bell is about to toll."

I gulped down my drink, then stood up and, taking Ben's drink, set them down. I took his hands and pulled him closer.

"Well, hello," Ben said, happily surprised. The crowd behind us began the countdown.

Ten, nine, eight, seven, six, five, four, three, two, one. Happy new year!

We shared a perfect kiss as streamers of all colors fell around us, the sound of noisemakers deafening. I looked up into Ben's blue eyes. "Happy New Year, Mr. Dalton."

"Happy New Year to my favorite news story of 1963." He leaned down and kissed me again. What a great way to start a new year.

When we pulled away, I looked at the surrounding revelers. "Nineteen sixty-four. New job. New president. A new start."

Acknowledgements

I would like to give my thanks to my uncle Donald D. Trent, an Illinois State Police Officer, who kindly spent time with me to tell me about life as a cop in 1963. Sadly, my uncle passed before the publication of If I Had a Hammer and I treasure the short time we had discussing the book.

I would also like thank my editor Shawn Simmons and my agent Dawn Dowdle who invested their time in me and my writing.

Finally, I would like to thank the ladies in my critique group who spent countless Monday evenings telling me what I did wrong and praising what I did right.

You may think writing a book involves one person, but it is often a collection of information, help along the way, and love from others.

About the Author

Teresa Trent is the author of over 15 books. She started writing cozy mysteries with the Pecan Bayou and Piney Woods Mystery Series. She mainly sets her stories in different geographical areas of Texas and The Swinging Sixties historical series is set just north of Dallas, starting in 1962. You might think with so many books set in the Lone Star state, she was born there, but no. She has lived all over the world, thanks to her father's career in the army. After living in Texas for twenty-five years, she's finally put down roots.

Teresa is a hybrid author, self-publishing early in her career, which led her to traditional publishing with Level Best Books and Camel Press. She is the author of several short stories that have appeared in a host of anthologies. Teresa publishes the blog and podcast, **Books to the Ceiling** at https://teresatrent.blog where she loves to read the book excerpts of other writers and share in the writing community.

Teresa is a member of Sisters in Crime and lives in Houston, Texas with her husband and son.

SOCIAL MEDIA HANDLES:
FACEBOOK:https://www.facebook.com/teresatrentmysterywriter
TWITTER: https://twitter.com/ttrent_cozymys
BLOG: https://teresatrent.blog/ (Books to the Ceiling)

WEBSITE: http://teresatrent.com

GOODREADS:https://www.goodreads.com/author/show/5219581.Teresa_Trent

INSTAGRAM:https://www.instagram.com/teresatrent_cozymys/

BOOKBUB: https://www.bookbub.com/profile/teresa-trent

AUTHOR WEBSITE:

https://teresatrent.com

Also by Teresa Trent

The Twist and Shout Murder

www.ingramcontent.com/pod-product-compliance
Lightning Source LLC
Chambersburg PA
CBHW030427120726
47903CB00003B/838